Killing Time

Tony McFadden

DEDICATION

For my partner for over thirty years, Linda.

DISCLAIMER

While I haven't confirmed this directly with the Detroit Police Department, I do not believe that they support the use of time travel. Also, the Detroit Police Department recently amalgamated their numerous Precincts to fewer, and larger, Districts. I've knowingly kept the Precincts intact.

ACKNOWLEDGMENTS

Writing is *not* a solitary endeavor.

Many thanks to the Northern Beaches Writers'
Group for their critique, and my Beta Readers
(Steven, Kay, Al, and Joyce).

Your input is greatly appreciated.

Chapter 1

Alex Wheeler slammed the van door shut, the kid under his arm screaming his head off.

"Shut up, ya fucking punk. We're miles from anyone. You're wasting your breath." He smacked the kid on the side of the head and grinned. "Not that anyone's gonna hear you out here."

The seven-year-old boy grabbed at Wheeler's arm, sobs wracking his chest. "Lemme go."

Wheeler adjusted the kid and walked up the back steps of an old farmhouse. "Watkins bettera been right." He rested his hand on the doorknob for a second, then gave it a turn. It opened, hinges screaming with rust. "Fuckin' A."

Wheeler walked into the kitchen and tried a faucet.

Rusty water poured out. "Gotta deep well, I guess. Finest kind." He turned off the faucet, dropped the boy and grabbed him by the arm. "You need ta clean up, punk. Everything's gonna be cool."

The boy kicked out at Wheeler. "I wanna go home."

Wheeler laughed. "Right. In the fucking tub, boy." He pushed the bathroom door open and threw the boy in. "Ya got a choice. Get undressed, or I do it for ya."

Detective Debra Collins rolled south, her department Buick fogging up. "Son of a bitch, piece of shit car." She rolled down the driver's window and flicked the fan on high. A stiff, cold breeze blew in from the east and the Great Lakes. "Winter's going to be a bitch this year."

She finger-combed her short blond hair, then scrolled through the numbers on her phone, picked one out and dialled. "Geezer, how far south?"

"Collins? You ain't paid me for the last time I gave you info."

"I'm good for it, Geez. You're my best CI. My favorite, even."

"I can smell bullshit all the way over here." Geezer paused for a minute, and Collins upped the volume on her phone.

"Geez? There's a kid involved, remember?"

"Yeah, yeah. I heard about five miles. You alone?"

"Five miles. Thanks."

The boy pushed himself into a corner of the tub, sitting in his underwear in the cold, rusty water.

"Good boy. Keep your fuckin' mouth shut." Wheeler stood in front of the bathroom mirror, looking at himself. He scraped at the stubble on his chin and looked at the boy in the mirror.

"You know what a Baker's Dozen is, boy?"

Wheeler turned to the tub and kneeled in front of it in a pool of water. He reached for the boy, who shoved himself further into the corner.

"Thirteen. You're my lucky thirteen."

Collins passed a tree-lined driveway, stopped and slowly backed up. The ass-end of a white van poked out from behind a weather-beaten farmhouse. She squinted, read the licence plate number and compared it to the number on her pad of paper. "Shit." She grabbed the mic off the dash. "Dispatch, Detective Collins. I've got Wheeler's van. Shit-brown house about five miles south of the overpass, on Wilkins Road."

She released the mic and listened to static for a second. *"Roger, Detective. Backup is about ten minutes out. Please hold for their arrival."*

Collins dropped the mic on the seat. "Like I've got ten minutes."

She eased the door open and stepped into the cold. "I'm retiring to Arizona. This is ridiculous." Collins removed her service revolver from its holster and eased down the drive, keeping in the tree cover. The gravel crunched underfoot. Her breath fogged the air.

The stillness of the early frost brought back old memories of campfires, crisp apples and mugs of hot chocolate and marshmallows.

Very old memories.

She eased up to the front of the house and crouched down below the eye-line of the front window. Noise came from the back, on the right side of the house, clear as a bell in the crisp air.

She duck-walked under the windows to that side of the house, stopping under the window producing the most noise. Slowly easing upright, she peeked in. Wheeler was there, back to the window, trying to grab the little boy in the tub.

Collins gripped her revolver tighter and ran to the back of the house. The door was partially open, the screen door hanging off its hinges. She stepped onto the porch, walking along the edge of the stairs to avoid squeaks. She pushed the door open with the barrel of her revolver, wincing at the squeal of the rusty hinge. Splashing noises echoed down the hallway.

Collins pushed into the kitchen, swept it quickly. Nobody there, and nobody expected. Wheeler was a loner.

She sidled down the hallway against the wall. The splashing noise grew louder.

"Fuck off, ya little shit. Stop struggling." Wheeler sounded like he was enjoying himself.

Collins pulled the hammer back on the revolver and spun into the bathroom.

"Freeze, asshole, or I'll drop you."

Wheeler was crouched over the tub. He froze for a second, then grabbed the boy and pulled his small frame in front of him, using him as a shield.

"Detective Collins. What the hell you doing, ruining my fun?" Wheeler looked past her, then back at the detective. "All by yourself?"

The boy whimpered, shivering and dripping water on the floor.

Wheeler put his hand over the boy's mouth and nose. "You know I like playing with them a bit longer than this. Back off, or he'll die faster."

Collins looked into the boy's eyes, filled with fear and slowly rolling back. She shifted her gaze to Wheeler. "You think I'll just leave?" She lowered her revolver, smiled at Wheeler and shot him in the foot.

Wheeler screamed and threw the boy at Collins. She caught him and landed on her ass in the water. Wheeler kicked at her and tried to get to the window.

Collins scrambled to her feet, grabbed her revolver off the floor and pushed the boy behind her. "Keep going. I'll just shoot you in the head."

Wheeler stopped, raising his hands. "You won't do that. Youse a cop."

"You were trying to escape. Maybe one in the gut. Let you bleed out."

She took a step backwards and bumped into the boy. He grabbed her leg. Collins reached back and gave his arm a gentle squeeze. "Maybe not in front of the kid."

Detective Sam Hastings cranked the wheel on his

department-issue sedan and threw gravel as he careened down the driveway. Uniforms followed. He ran up the front steps and hammered on the door.

"Police. Open up."

"Kick it down, Hastings. I can't really move right now."

"Collins?"

"Who in the hell else would it be?"

Hastings leaned back and drove his size-twelve foot into the door just below the knob. The frame splintered, and he and the uniforms streamed in.

Collins sat on a ratty sofa in the living room, the small boy wrapped in her jacket on her left.

Face down on the mildewed carpet was Wheeler, hands cable-tied behind his back. Collins snugged the boy in tight. Her right hand was rock steady, her revolver trained on Wheeler's head.

"Okay, Collins. We've got it from here. You're an idiot for going in alone."

She rotated her gun hand counter-clockwise, still

trained on Wheeler's head, and looked at her watch. "It took you and your backup fifteen minutes to get here. The kid would have been—well, let's not talk about it in front of him."

Hastings holstered his sidearm and scratched at the stubble on his chin. "Ya got a point. Great ending to your career, eh?"

Uniforms collected Wheeler and Collins finally lowered her arm. "All anticlimactic after this." She watched Wheeler struggle as he was led out. "Won't miss assholes like that, though." She looked at the boy beside her and gave him a motherly squeeze. "I think we need to get you home, kiddo."

Chapter 2

Hastings pulled off the I-75 to a plot of land under an overpass. Cars and tractor-trailers screamed by, unbothered by the cop car's flashing lights. It was a small triangle of land where I-75 intersected with State Road 10. Burger wrappers, old pop cans and other trash littered the sparse, uncut grass.

"Here?"

Hastings turned off the ignition. "Here." He opened the door, a cold blast of air blowing the heat out of the car. "Couldn't find the place first time I looked for it."

She looked at the file. "So why'd Dempsey dump this on you?"

"The kid left on his honeymoon." Hastings stepped into the crisp air and snugged his jacket around his tall frame. He leaned in the car and took the file from Collins. "You coming?"

"Bloody cold out there."

"You wanted to get away from your desk. Here you are."

"True. Nice to be out in the field."

Hastings chuckled. "Yeah. You looked pathetic."

"Killing time chewing through cold cases wasn't how I planned on spending my last two months as a cop." Collins shoved her hands in her pocket. "So this is where the body was found?"

Hastings opened the file folder and took out a picture. He looked at the photos, then at the environs and moved about ten feet toward the center of the overgrown piece of dirt. "About here. Almost directly under the overpass."

"When was the body found?"

"Three days ago. Trucker called it in. Didn't hang around."

Collins nodded and walked slowly around the area,

head down, searching. "Killed somewhere else."

"Yeah. No blood."

Collins pointed at some dirt near the curb. "Tire marks here. No sign of a struggle. Who was it?"

Hastings flipped to the front page of the file. "Asshole called Phil Packer. Early thirties. Not a smart man. Had a bunch of run-ins with the vice boys and was a suspect in a couple of drive-by shootings."

"Poor guy. Probably went through school as 'fudge packer'.

"Poor guy? Nah. Thought we had him on the drive-bys but he slipped on a technicality."

"Gang-bangers?"

"Who, his targets? Usually. But last time around he caught a young girl and her newborn. Killed the mother and the baby was killed in the car accident after the shooting." Hastings pointed at the ground in front of him. "This was the best place for him."

"Maybe six feet under."

Hastings shook his head. "On the surface. Let the

scavengers feed on him."

Collins cocked an eyebrow. "Vigilante as all get out. Knew I liked you."

Collins walked to the far side of the lot, scouring the ground.

"What you lookin' for?"

Collins continued walking, head down. "Not sure." She took her hands out of her pockets and blew on them. "Have we been here before?"

"You've been at your desk for the past two weeks, since the Wheeler bust, scavenging cold cases. Before that? I don't think so. Maybe. Why?"

Collins stopped walking and looked past Hastings. "Up the hill. That service station on the other side of the highway. Used to be a Texaco, right?"

"I think so."

"Son of a bitch. Ruiz was dumped here." Collins walked across the lot toward Hastings. "What are the odds?"

"Who the hell is Ruiz?"

"The cold case I'm looking at right now. Garcia Ruiz. Seventeen years ago. Thought I recognized this place. Been looking at those photos for days now. He was shot, twice in the chest, and dumped here. Never found the place he was actually killed."

"Same place, both dumped, both killed the same way, somewhere else."

Collins looked back up at the service station again. "They'd have security cameras."

Hastings shook his head. "Checked. No dice. Covers the pumps and the interior of the station. Nothing even remotely close to this overpass."

Hastings walked back to his car, Collins beside him. "You think maybe someone's been out of circulation for a while and is now just getting back in the game?"

"Worth looking at. We can compare notes back at the station." Collins jumped in the car, rubbing her hands. "Start the damned thing and turn on the heater."

Hastings tossed the Parker file at Collins and got in.

"Look at this again. See if anything sparks a memory."

"If you turn the heater on." Collins grabbed the file and flipped pages with frozen fingers. The top couple of pages contained the medical examiner's report. She licked a finger and clumsily flipped to the second page. "Heater, pup, or I'll slap you with my ice hands."

"You'd need a step ladder to reach my face, granny. Give it a second. It's an old car."

Collins flipped through the file. "Not a lot to work with. This is really thin. There's nothing in here."

Hastings nodded. "Need to find where he was killed. Very little trace on the body, and ballistics were useless."

Collins read from the file. "One through and through and one dug out, presumably by the killer. Find the kill scene and you might find the through and through."

"Yeah. Got to find the kill scene, first. No luck so far. Like you said, damned little trace on the body."

Collins mobile phone rang. She looked at the

display and swore. "Captain Barnes. Shit." She muted the ring and slid the phone back in her pocket.

"Oh, you didn't." Hastings shook his head. "You know he's gonna—"

Hastings phone rang. He grunted and answered. "Captain. What can I do for you?"

"Put it on speaker."

Hastings pushed the button. "You're on speaker, Cap. What's up?"

"Collins, why didn't you answer your phone?"

Hastings smiled and handed the phone to Collins.

She placed it on the console between them. "Hey, Barnes. It's cold out here. Did you call?"

"You know damned well I did."

"I didn't hear it ring. You hear it ring, Hastings? I'm getting old, you know. Advanced hearing loss."

"Bullshit, and Hastings will lie for you. Get back to the station, now."

"There's a reason I took Collins out with me, Cap."

"I don't care. Get back here, now."

The call dropped and Collins handed the phone back to Hastings. "Thanks for backing me. Cap's got his panties in a twist over nothing."

"What reason did he give for benching you?"

"Other than the fact my retirement is in two months? Six weeks now, actually. No real reason makes sense. The Wheeler catch was good. Nothing out of the ordinary there."

"You did shoot him in the foot."

"Yeah. Nothing out of the ordinary." She shook her head. "I was an ounce of pressure away from splattering his brains all over the bathroom wall."

"I'm not sure I could have held off."

"The kid. He was freaked out enough. Didn't need to completely ruin his life. It's going to be hard enough as it is for the little guy."

Hastings sat silent for a couple of seconds. "I never pictured you as maternal, but that kid snugged up under your arm when I got there, well, that was something else."

"And my service revolver trained on Wheeler's skull. Real homey."

Hastings shrugged. "True. So you never had kids?"

"Long story."

"Not too long, I hope. You're gone in six weeks."

"Or less. I don't think I can handle six more weeks on a desk."

"Don't cut your retirement short. You're going to live a long time, as tough and ornery as you are. You're going to need the money."

"Bitch."

Hastings laughed and pulled into the station parking lot. "You didn't answer me about the kids. You got grown ones hiding somewhere?"

She took a deep breath and slowly let it out. "It never happened for us. And when Larry kicked the bucket fifteen years ago, I had no interest in starting new with someone else." She looked over at Hastings, over six feet tall and in fantastic shape for a forty-year-old, and smiled. "But I might make an exception if you ever split up with what's her name."

"I'm twenty years younger than you. Maybe you can adopt me."

"Bitch."

Hastings tipped his head back and laughed. "I'm going to miss you." He turned off the car and popped the door.

"Don't go getting all maudlin, pup. Jesus, do I have to go out there? It's bloody cold out."

"It's only October."

Collins stood and stretched. She slammed the car door shut and shoved her hands in her pockets. "January, February is going to be a bitch."

"You'll be retired. Head to Florida and come back when it's melting back here."

"Too humid. Arizona, maybe."

"With all the blue-haired ladies? You'll rule the roost."

Collins hunched against the cold wind and walked to the station. "Block the wind for me, will ya?"

Hastings pulled her close and shielded her. "We get in there, show me the Ruiz file."

Chapter 3

Collins and Hastings walked past the Desk Sergeant, flashed their identification cards and entered the chaos.

Collins shrugged off her jacket and waded through the desks toward hers. "Heads up, Hastings. Your nine-o'clock."

Barnes, looking like the aged ex-football player he was, pushed through the crowd and intercepted Collins before she got to her desk.

"Detective, you're not Hastings' partner. Please keep your focus on the cold cases I've tasked you to work on."

"Hey, Cap, relax," said Hastings. "One of the cold cases had striking similarities to the active dump I'm working on."

Collins dropped into her seat and lifted her feet onto her desk. "Take it easy, Hastings. I can fend for myself. Barnes, I've got more experience than you and Hastings put together. Well, almost. If I want to get out from behind my desk once in a while, I will." She swung her legs off the desk, grabbed a file and opened it. "This Ruiz guy was dumped in the same place, seventeen years ago, killed in the same way."

Hastings took the file and flipped it open to the photos. "We think they may be connected. A lot of similarities. Coincidences-"

"-don't exist." Collins looked at her nails for a second.

Barnes looked over Hastings' shoulder. "Don't care, Collins. You're chained to your desk, working on the backlog of cold cases."

"Something I said? Jesus, Barnes. I'm wasting time here."

Barnes placed his hands on her desk and leaned

forward. "You shot an unarmed man."

"In the foot."

"Stop. You shot an unarmed man. I'll grant you perhaps I would have done the same. Worse, maybe. But the bleeding-heart lawyer types are having a field day with this."

Collins sat forward. "It was a good bust."

"Yeah, yeah. Relax. It was a great bust. I'd like to buy the CI who led you to him a very large drink. In the meantime, stay off the street, below the radar and clean up some of these cold cases for me. Whatever you do, stay away from anything to do with the Wheeler case."

Barnes turned on his heel and walked back up the stairs to his office.

Collins watched him leave. "So, what ya think?"

Hastings flipped through a couple of pages of the Ruiz case file. "I'm taking it. Almost identical."

Collins smiled, stood and lifted the case file off her desk. "All yours. Where do you want it?"

Hastings leaned back in his chair and pointed at his desk. "Find a place. What are these burn marks on the body?"

"Didn't get that far. Why?"

"Same ones on Packer. Sort of the same. Strange."

"Enjoy. I'm going to go find myself another one to work."

Hastings nodded without looking up. He had both medical reports on his desk, side by side.

Collins scrolled through a list of cold cases on her computer terminal, wrote down a case number and headed back to the evidence locker.

Collins' flicked through the ME report of the fourth case on her desk and swore.

"What's up, Granny? You're drowning in paper over there."

"Ruiz help you any?"

Hastings shrugged and held up a photo from the file. "These burn marks. Same in both. Never mentioned in the news reports about Ruiz, so I think it's definitely the same guy. Not much else other than that, though. Why? What you got?"

"Three more with extremely similar markers. All were dumped within a mile of each other, and all were shot twice. Some in the chest, some in the back."

Hastings dropped the picture on his desk. "Burn marks?"

"Hard to say. On some of them, yes. Some of the autopsies were pretty shitty."

Hastings walked over to Collins' desk and sat beside it. "You've got four cases there."

"One of them wasn't shot. Header off a building. The other three, though, you can have them. All the same guy, I'd bet money on it."

"Fuck."

"Yeah. We've had a slow-burn serial killer right under our noses."

"How far back?

Collins checked a file. "Earliest is 1977. Were you

even born then?"

"Just. I was two." Hastings rubbed his face. "So you're clearing your cold cases by dumping them on me? Well done, champ. Barnes needs to see this."

"You go show him." She grabbed her jacket off the back of her chair. "I'm going home.

Collins entered the station the next morning, and into a sea of suits. The glass-walled conference room, rarely used, was in the process of being converted into a War Room of some sort. Whiteboards, easels and assorted laptops and PCs were installed and a shiny crew of young federal agents worked with a sense of purpose Collins hadn't felt in years.

Hastings stood outside the new War Room with his hands on his hips.

"What the hell is this," asked Collins.

He looked down at her and then back to the room. "Full court press from the fibbies. I haven't seen this amount of heat, ever. This is like Zodiac level stuff."

"What's Barnes said about it?"

Hastings pointed up the stairs. Captain Barnes and a very impressive-looking man in a suit and tie were walking down from Barnes's office side by side and talking animatedly. "He's said nothing to us yet. But I expect we'll hear something shortly."

Collins hung her jacket on the back of her chair and sat. "He's got to be loving this."

Barnes reached the last step of the stairs and stopped, slightly elevated compared to the rest of the room. He cleared his throat. "Excuse me, everybody." He waited until the dull roar in the squad room eased off. "Gentlemen. And ladies. Detective Collins, in her usual way, has managed to make our lives all that more complicated."

Friendly jeers and catcalls flooded the squad room. Collins smiled, raised her right hand as far as she could and gave the collective audience the bird.

"Very nice, Collins. In her quest to close out as many cold cases as possible before she retires, the good detective has found three -"

"Four," interrupted Hastings.

"Four cases that have markers extremely similar to a recent case Hastings has pulled. It looks like, for at least the past thirty years, we've had a serial killer working our fine city."

He placed his hand on the shoulder of the man beside him. "This is Special Agent Paul Wilson of the Federal Bureau of Investigation, D.C. office. He and his friends will be running the show. He'll pick from our numbers those he wants on the task force. You will do everything you can to assist them in bringing this ratbag to justice."

Barnes slapped Wilson on the shoulder and stepped to one side, letting Wilson take the floor.

"Thanks to Detective Hastings, we have a chance at shutting down someone who has killed at least five times over the past thirty years."

Collins leaned close to Hastings. "The guy's an idiot. Closer to forty years. But at least you're getting the laurels for this."

"I'll let him know it was you."

"Oh, fuck no. My career is ended. It'll do me no good. You take it. Maybe it'll get you an extra salary bump come review time." She chuckled. "Did you hear Barnes? That was funny."

"What?"

"He's as convincing saying "ratbag" as my dear departed granny would have been rapping some Eminem. The stick is so far up his ass, I don't know how he actually bends."

Wilson wrapped up whatever he was saying, and he and his agents filed back into the War Room. He barked orders at some of the junior agents, and case information started populating the whiteboards. Collins nodded toward the glass-walled room. "You think I'll get on this?"

Hastings scratched at his chin. "You should. But you won't. Barnes'll block it. I can't tell if he's concerned for your safety or hates you."

"If it wasn't for me, despite what the Fed said, there wouldn't be a task force."

Collins turned back to her desk, Hastings behind her.

"You'd think you were taking credit for the killings."

Collins lifted the one remaining evidence box onto her desk and flipped off the top. She took out the file and flipped it open. "At least I've still got this one."

"What is it?"

"Oldest in the pile. Some dude named Carl Smith. Real name, as far as I can tell."

"What's his story?"

"Took a header off a building in August 1976."

"Sounds like a suicide."

"He was chased off."

Hastings wandered back to his desk and dropped in his chair. "Good citizen?"

"Nope. Dodged a vehicular homicide case. Killed a mom and her daughter while he was DUI."

Chapter 4

Collins stopped in front of an aging apartment building in an area struggling its way out of the recession. The cars on the street were old, but well maintained. The building itself, seven stories tall and made of brick sometime in the 1920s, looked like an old dowager trying to hold on to her looks for as long as she could.

She wrapped her jacket tight against the cold, slid the case file under her arm and pushed the Superintendent's buzzer. "Detective Collins here. I'd like to speak to you about a murder that happened about forty years ago."

The door buzzed without a verbal response. She pulled it open and stepped into the warmth. A short, borderline obese man stepped out of a door on the ground floor. "Detective Collins? I am Bart Fredricks, like of Hollywood. I'm to understand you're here to talk about the Smith death?" He walked toward her with his hand extended.

Collins shook his hand. "You're still the Super after forty years? That's a strange stroke of luck for me."

"I'm also the owner of the building. The other tenants don't know. Probably. At least, they play along with me if they do."

"I don't understand."

"I put things off by saying I need to discuss with the owner, and he's out of town, or he won't pay for a certain thing. It's harmless. But yes, I'm still here. Smith was a strange bird."

"I'd like to see where he jumped."

Bart looked at Collins for a second, then at the stairs. "We, um, don't have an elevator. We'll have to walk the seven flights."

"Okay." Collins smiled and walked toward the

stairs. "I assume the roof access is locked?"

"Shit. Yeah. Hang on." Bart followed Collins to the stairs and started climbing. The smell of fresh roast coffee from one of the apartments suffused the stairwell.

"Do you have a high tenant turnover?"

"No," Bart wheezed. "The average occupancy length of the twenty-four in here now is something like five or six years."

"What about the Smith guy? Had he been here long before he jumped?"

"A couple of years. I hope you don't take this the wrong way, but he saved me a ton of trouble."

"How's that?"

"I was preparing the paperwork to evict him."

"Didn't pay the rent?"

"He paid on time. The problem was his parties. Too many, too loud and they lasted too long. I had a lot of complaints. He was the reason I added a noise clause to the tenancy agreement."

Collins rounded the stairs toward the third floor. "But he jumped before you had to kick him out?" She took off her jacket and slung it over her shoulder.

Bart grabbed onto the handrail and pulled himself upward. "Yeah. I was glad. I didn't think I really had a leg to stand on, kicking him out. Solved a lot of problems. And saved me money in legal fees."

"Forty years ago, and you're still fretting over it."

"Not my proudest moment, telling my lawyer he didn't have to proceed 'cause the guy killed himself. He thought I was to blame."

"Who, the lawyer?"

"Said I drove Smith to his death."

"Wow. Asshole lawyers." Collins rounded the landing, heading toward the fifth floor. "How do people get their groceries up here?"

"We're a fit lot."

Collins looked over her shoulder at the portly man and smiled. "Okay. So Smith was a drunk and an asshole, paid his rent on time. What else can you tell me? Any enemies you know of?"

"Other than his neighbors? Nah. I can't think of any. I don't know if he gambled. If he owed money, it didn't affect his paying rent. The only trouble he was in was that accident he had while he was drunk. He got off somehow. House arrest, maybe."

"No. Wasn't house arrest. Free and clear."

Collins walked the last flight to the roof access. She stood to one side so Bart could unlock the door. "You coming out with me?"

"Yeah." He held the door for her to pass. Sweat soaked his face and neck. He had sweat rings under his arms and under his chest and down his back.

"It's going to be fucking cold out there."

Bart smiled. "I'm insulated."

Collins stepped through and pulled on her jacket. Bart followed. He grabbed a concrete block and propped the door open as she slowly walked to the edge.

Collins looked back at him. "Here, right?"

"That side, yeah." He took a handkerchief from his pocket and wiped the sweat off his face and neck. Steam rose from his scalp. "Hey, Detective Collins, could you not stand so close to the edge? I can't afford an increase in insurance premiums." He folded the handkerchief and wiped his hands. "Once was enough."

Collins continued to stare over the edge while she talked. "Forty years ago."

"Still. The paperwork."

"I'm not going to fall." She stood upright and consulted the case file. She flicked through the pages until she found a crime scene photo taken from the rooftop. She examined the picture, looked over the edge and took three steps to her right. She held the photo out, obscuring the present reality, and then removed it. She was in the right place.

"So he just jumped?"

Bart shuffled a little closer. "Like he thought he could fly."

"You saw him hit the ground?"

"Oh, hell no. I saw him jump. I wasn't close enough to the edge to see him land." He paused. "Heard him hit, though."

Collins examined the wall around the edge of the rooftop. It stood almost two feet high. "Easy enough to jump over this. It's not very safe."

"Tenants don't normally have access to the roof. I've got the only key."

"You take vacation, right?"

"Sure. Going to Florida in February."

"And you have a trusted tenant take Super duties while you're gone?"

"Limited duties. I guess."

"And you give them the keys. At least half of your tenants will have keys to the roof. There are fresh cigarette butts out here, and the trashcan in the corner has some beer bottles in it. How did Smith get on the roof to jump in the first place?"

Bart was silent, thinking.

"I'm not coming down on you. There are no new charges, if that's what you're worried about. Just opening your eyes a bit. Change the lock, maybe."

"Shit."

Collins walked back from the ledge and stood face-to-face with Bart. "Maybe you were up here doing maintenance when he ran up? The door was unlocked, maybe?"

Bart shook his head, his jowls in an angry dance. "No, I was chasing the woman who was chasing him."

Collins looked pointedly at Bart's gut.

"I was a lot thinner back then."

"Sure you were. Tell me about the woman. Why was she chasing Smith?"

Bart walked back to the door. "Hell if I know. And I didn't get a good look at her. She was wearing one of those track jackets with its hood up."

"In August."

Bart nodded. "I know. That's why I noticed her. Followed her up the stairs and when she started chasing Smith, I chased her."

Collins stood by the propped open door and looked around. "How is it you chased them up on the roof and she managed to escape? This is the only way off the roof. Other than the path Smith took."

Bart kicked the block out of the way and followed Collins into the building. "She jolted me."

"What, like a cross-check?"

Bart locked the roof access door and followed her down the stairs. "No, not like that."

"A push? Kick? Slap? What?"

"Jolted me. Zapped me. Damnedest thing."

Collins stopped on the stairs and turned. "What, like a Taser?"

Bart snapped his fingers and nodded. "Exactly."

Collins continued walking down the stairs. "Not a Taser, though, because they didn't exist in 1976. Hell, we didn't get them at the department until, what, 2005? No, 2006."

"Then it was something that looked and felt very

much like a Taser. I had burn marks for years. Faded now, but I'll never forget how it felt."

Bart and Collins walked the rest of the stairs in silence, the sounds and smells of the apartment building filling the void. Somewhere, someone was cooking peanut butter cookies, and someone else was working out to an exercise video. The coffee smell was still strong.

Collins took a card out of her wallet and handed it to Bart. "I appreciate the time. It was very helpful. If you remember anything else, please give me a call, okay?"

Bart took the card and slid it into his wallet. "It's been forty years. I doubt I'll remember anything other than what I've already told you."

"Maybe so. But if you do."

Chapter 5

Detective Collins drove back through the city, mulling over her visit with Bart. So much didn't make sense.

She parked outside of the station and walked in, deep in thought. She flung her jacket over the back of her chair, looked in her coffee cup, scowled and headed into the small kitchen. She walked past the War Room, dirty cup in hand, and stopped by the door. The FBI agents and local officers were in full swing, the ambient noise significantly louder than outside the room. She shook her head and walked into the kitchen.

Hastings was already in there, making a cup of coffee. "You're back. Any joy?"

Collins shook her head. "Strangeness. Small

woman chases large man off a roof. You'd think he'd try fighting back. By Bart's description, the vic outweighed the woman by at least fifty pounds." She looked up at Hastings. "It would be like me chasing you off a roof. Sound plausible?"

"Bart?"

"The Super-slash-owner of the building. Looks a lot like Boss Hogg, but fatter." Collins grinned. "Made him walk up seven flights of stairs."

"You're going to miss this."

"Don't remind me."

She scrubbed the coffee ring out of her cup and nodded back toward the War Room. "Why aren't you in there with the winners and grinners?"

"The Feds have it well in hand. They're mapping all the dump sites in an attempt to find a locus for the killer."

Collins slid a pod into the coffee machine. "Would work better if they mapped the actual kill sites." She took her cup and followed him out of the kitchen back to their desks.

"That it would. " Hastings cleared his throat and placed his coffee cup on his desk. "I tried telling them, but they aren't listening to me. That Wilson guy doesn't think much of me, for some reason." He shrugged. "But what do we know, eh?"

Collins sat and started transcribing notes from the visit. "Less and less each day, I'm afraid." She looked up. "He said he was jolted. Zapped."

Hastings dropped in his chair. "Who, the dead guy? How would you know?"

"No. Bart. In 1970-whatever it was. Thirty-odd years before *we* got them, he says the woman chasing the vic zapped him with a Taser to stop him from stopping her."

Hastings raised his eyebrows. "Not likely. Bad memories. The bane of our existence."

"Same thing in the case file. First on the scene interviewed him and wrote, and I quote, 'The lady zapped me with something that felt like a really strong electric shock. I fell to the ground and couldn't move my muscles for at least ten minutes. Like I was paralyzed or something.'" She flipped the page back again. "Sure sounds like how I'd describe the results of getting tagged if I'd never heard of a Taser before."

Hastings was glued to his monitor.

"Hastings? You awake?"

Hastings grunted and pointed at his computer screen. "I take it you haven't seen this yet?"

"We were talking about impossible Tasers, pup. You're kinda young for Alzheimer's."

"No. You gotta see this. Sorry. It's about Wheeler."

Collins rolled her chair across to Hastings' desk. "What about that fuck? He get hit by a bus?"

Hastings wheeled back and let her at his machine.

He had a local news website open. The large, bold headline read: PEDOPHILE RELEASED ON TECHNICALITY. Below the headline was a picture of the greasy-haired, balding Wheeler with a shit-eating grin on his face as he left the courthouse.

"I'm really sorry." Hastings reached over and placed his hand on her arm.

"Son of a motherfucking bitch. What happened?"

Hastings sighed. "It wasn't anything you did, as far as I can tell from the report. The prosecutor messed up. It happens."

Collins kicked her chair back to her desk and drove a heel into the bottom drawer, leaving a dent. "Son. Of. A BITCH." She slammed her fist on her desk.

She took a deep breath. "So we grab him again and start over." She pushed back and stood. "Coming? I've got to find him."

"Sit. Double jeopardy." He walked to her desk and sat on the corner. "Don't worry. He'll do something stupid again."

"Yeah. He will. And the next time he does something stupid, another kid will be brutalized. This is abso-fucking-lutely horseshit."

Collins slammed the lid on the cold case file box, grabbed her jacket and kicked her chair to one side. "I need to get some air."

Barnes walked down the stairs from his office and watched Collins leave. He nodded at Hastings. "What the hell's going on with her?"

Hastings rotated his monitor so Barnes could see it. "Ah, shit. What do you think she's going to do?"

"What are you thinking?" Hastings pulled the monitor back. "She's just walking it off." He pointed at the screen. "Wouldn't it bend you a bit?"

"Yeah. Jesus."

"You want me to follow her?"

Barnes shook his head. "Let her blow off steam."

Collins showed her credentials at the department firing range, hung up her jacket and inspected her service revolver.

"You here for certification, Detective? You're not on the list." The Sergeant flipped through the papers on his clipboard.

"Just keeping the rust off." Collins placed her service revolver on the counter and retrieved a pair of ear protection muffs.

"You're not using the new FNS? What's wrong? Too much weapon for you?"

Collins looked at her revolver with a smile. "I'm outta here in a month or so. And I like my revolver. I've had it my entire career. And it doesn't jam like those semi-automatic pieces of crap do." Collins scribbled across the top of the target, pinned it to the runner and pressed the button, sending it to the back of the range.

"Hundred yards?"

Collins looked at the Sergeant. "*Keeping* the rust off. Not *knocking* the rust off." She held the earmuffs out from her ears and looked at the Sergeant. "Can I get some space?"

The Sergeant smiled and stepped back. "Have at it."

Collins adopted the Weaver stance and let six rounds go in rapid succession. She flipped open the cylinder, dropped the casings and used her speed-loader. She closed the cylinder and let six more rounds go.

"Fast."

Collins looked at the young Sergeant. "Practice makes perfect." She punched the button and reeled in the target. All twelve rounds formed a tight group in the groin area.

"Shooting low?"

Collins looked at the target and dropped it in the bin. "Exactly where I wanted them to be."

The Sergeant pulled the target out of the bin as Collins walked away. "I'm going to keep this, if that's okay?"

Collins waved without looking back.

The Sergeant flattened the folds out on a table. Across the top she had written "Wheeler".

Later, as the sun went down and the cold, October night blanketed the city, Collins parked in front of her apartment building after driving aimlessly for hours. She pulled her jacket tight around her and walked up the front steps.

It was still a pretty good neighborhood. The building owner kept the place well-maintained, and the neighbors kept their lawns mowed. A few places tended to party a little louder and a little later than she'd like, but she recognized this was just another sign of her increasing age.

And she hated it.

She navigated the front door lock and apartment lock and once again regretted the solitary life she led. The apartment was dark and cold. She flicked on the lights, kicked the radiator and gave its knob a twist. She hung her jacket on the back of the chair in the kitchen and plugged in the kettle.

While they warmed up, both the kettle and the apartment, she rummaged through the fridge looking for something to eat. She slammed the fridge door shut, opened an app on her phone and ordered a pizza.

Like usual.

She dropped in the recliner in front of the television with her cup of tea, waiting for the delivery of double pepperoni and extra cheese, and turned on the news.

Wheeler's release led the stories.

Chapter 6

Entire neighborhoods were in disrepair, the owners walking away from their houses years ago, and the banks doing nothing to capitalize on their newly acquired properties. And it wouldn't have made any difference if they did want to capitalize, nobody had the money to buy homes any more. Those who might have, well, they didn't trust the economy. Not yet.

Among the run-down, decrepit houses on this block stood a two-bedroom bungalow with an attached, single-car garage still in good condition. The lawn was autumn brown, but it was recently mowed and edged. The flowerbeds were empty, but it was coming on winter. In the spring, there would be flowers.

Among the other houses in the neighbourhood, this

one stood out, with relatively fresh paint, an off-white, and clean yard.

The windows had wrought iron railings in front of them. By some miracle, the glass wasn't broken.

A mouse scuttered along the baseboard in the living room, heading down the hall to the kitchen on the right. The carpet was old, but not very worn. The house was clean but clearly unoccupied.

The kitchen cupboard doors hung open. The sink had rust stains, and the linoleum was old, dated, and cracked in a couple of places.

The refrigerator and stove were a horrible avocado green, popular in the seventies. The stovetop elements were the old spiraled ones, gray now, and coated with dust.

Down the hallway on the left was a small bathroom and two bedrooms. The bathroom was in the same state as the kitchen—old, dusty and in marginal shape.

The smaller bedroom looked almost pristine by comparison. With no closets or wardrobes, all left to decay was the carpet. And it was getting close. It was once shag, but it had flattened with wear. The window was covered with old metal venetian blinds.

The second bedroom, at the back of the house, was larger and had a small walk-in closet. The carpet was also threadbare, and the window was intact. A hole had been punched in the wall near the closet and repaired by a non-professional.

The closet door stood partly open. A rumble started in the floor, shaking a couple of the metal hangers hanging off the wooden rod. The wall at the back of the closet started slowly lowering, revealing a large glass dome sitting over an armchair.

When the wall had dropped out of sight, the thrumming noise increased, and electricity arced between the glass dome and the chair. The thrumming reached a crescendo as a figure slowly materialized under the glass.

Before the arcing completely stopped, the figure pulled the hood of her track jacket over her head, obscuring her face. The dome rose, and she stood, pulling on a pair of kid-leather gloves. She wore matching track pants and well-worn black tennis shoes.

She ducked under the rod, stepped out of the closet and lifted one of the hangers, activating a switch. The glass dome eased into place as the wall slowly rose, hiding her entry point.

She pulled the hanger back down into position and left the bedroom. She walked into the living room and peered through the venetian blinds. It was late, just after midnight.

She scanned the street outside the house. Nothing out of the ordinary, no cops, nobody paying any particular attention to one house among all the others.

A door in the wall between the first bedroom and the bathroom led to the garage. She opened it and walked confidently through the dark to the far side. She lifted up one of the shelves, activating another switch, and the garage floor lowered.

She spread her legs slightly, balancing against the movement. When the floor had lowered about three feet, a light came on below. She pulled the hood to shield her eyes from the brightness.

When the garage floor had dropped about eight feet it stopped. The Woman stepped off the floor and into a cavernous area at least twice the square footage of the house above her.

She pulled a tarp off a car, exposing a black 1967 El Camino in mint condition. She rolled the tarp into a ball and left it against the far wall. She brushed her gloved hand against the side of the car, caressing it, and slid into the driver's seat. The engine started on the first turn, the deep V-8 rumble echoing through the underground cave.

She backed the car onto the lowered garage floor, rolled down the driver's side window and poked at a red button on the wall. The floor rose, lifting her and the car into the garage.

When the floor stopped rising she pushed the garage

door opener hanging off her visor. The metal door rose slowly and she backed out of the garage into the crisp night air, pushing the button and closing the door behind her.

The Woman stopped the car in front of Collins' apartment. The street was still. The analog clock on the dash read 2:47. At this time of night, the world was asleep.

She stepped out of her car and pulled the hood over her head. She stopped at the front door and looked around, then took a key out of her pocket and opened the door.

The building was as quiet as it was outside. She stopped in front of Collins' apartment door and rested her hand on the knob. If the inside was latched with the security chain, she'd have to think of something else, but this would be the easiest way.

She unlocked the apartment door and carefully eased it open. It opened farther than a chain would allow. She smiled, partially in relief and partially with satisfaction.

Thirty seconds later she had what she needed. She left, locked the door behind her and drove off into the night.

Chapter 7

"So where did you go yesterday?" Hastings handed Collins a cup of coffee and followed her to her desk. "Are you okay?"

She held up an access card on a lanyard. "Spent thirty minutes looking for my pass this morning. Thirty God-damned minutes."

"You found it. Relax."

"No, I didn't. This is a temporary one. I'm going to have to rip the apartment apart tonight. I know I left it on the table by the front door. I'm positive."

"It'll be the last place you look."

"It always is." Collins looked across the squad room at the glass-walled War Room. The far wall was segmented into seven columns, with a picture of each victim at the top of each column. She squinted, but couldn't read the case details listed below each picture.

A large-scale map of the city stood on an easel, the dumpsites of the seven victims represented by pins. She shook her head and looked at Hastings. "What did you say?"

"You seem a little messed up. You okay?"

Collins took a sip of her coffee and considered the question. "Why wouldn't I be?"

Hastings looked at her a moment. "So, where did you go yesterday?"

"Shooting range. Blowing off steam. Honest, I'm fine." Collins flipped open a file and started reading the contents.

"New cold case file?"

"Nah. Wheeler file. Looking for something— anything—I might have missed."

"Double jeopardy, granny. Not even new evidence will put him away for the same crime. Give it a break."

"Can't hurt trying."

Hastings opened his mouth, shook his head and sat at his desk.

Collins looked over at him. He had turned on his monitor and was looking at something on his computer. She scribbled on a pad of paper, ripped off the piece and slid it into her pocket.

"You're tilting at windmills, granny."

Collins grunted, closed the Wheeler file and slid it to the back of her desk.

Hastings put his feet up on his desk. "So, the serial case. What ya think?"

Collins leaned back and rubbed her face. "I've got cold cases to worry about, with information from unreliable witnesses."

Hastings laughed and picked up the Packer file. "Since when have we had *reliable* witnesses?"

"Yeah, I'm trying to figure out old Bart. No way he could have been Tased in 1976. Wonder what it actually was." She returned to the medical report and sipped coffee as she read. After a few minutes her cup froze, half way to her mouth.

"You okay, granny? *Rigour mortis* set in?"

Collins set her coffee cup on her desk. "Maybe old Bart wasn't too far off. Look at these burn marks."

Hastings walked to Collins' desk and took the file. "What are you talking about? What burn marks?"

"On Smith's butt. Which is where he'd get tagged if he was running away." She handed the photo to Hastings and continued reading the file. "The M.E. mentioned it as a pair of burns." She flipped to the front of the report. "Shit. Dammit."

Hastings looked up from the photo. "What?"

"The M.E. was Pritchard. Died a few years ago."

Hastings grunted and returned to the photo. A pair of obvious burn marks were visible in the small of the back, just above the victim's left butt cheek. They were about an inch apart and fresh. "Nineteen seventy-six."

"I know. So tell me what it is." Collins grabbed the photo from Hastings. "Gimme."

She pushed past him and into the War Room. She looked around and picked out Special Agent Wilson. She marched up to him and poked a finger in his chest. He stood at least a foot taller than her.

"Hey, you. I need to see the medical examiner's photos of the victims' torsos."

Wilson looked down on her. "And you are who?"

Collins held his gaze for a few seconds and pushed past him.

He frowned and turned to follow her. "Hang on a second. What in the hell do you think you're doing?"

"Your job, apparently. I need torso photos for each of the victims."

"You're not on the task force. I'd recognize you. And I don't."

Collins held the photo in front of Wilson's face and jabbed a finger at the burn marks. "See these? The marks on his ass. Came from a Taser. Nineteen seventy-six. Don't say it's impossible. I know Taser burns when I see them. Looks like puncture wounds from the barbs mixed in with a cigarette burn. Very recognizable."

Wilson took the photos from Collins and examined it closely. "Maybe. Maybe not. The fact that this guy clearly wasn't shot and wasn't dumped some distance from his kill site lets me think this has absolutely nothing to do with our current serial case." He handed the photo back to Collins. "So get out of our way."

Collins shook her head and walked back to her desk. Hastings had a wry grin on his face. "What are you laughing at?"

"Windmills. Just relax and start easing into retirement. You've done way more than your fair share for the force. Let the young guys go at it."

"Ageist prick." But Collins couldn't help smiling back at him. "That guy's an idiot."

"Your case isn't compelling. Look at it from his point of view."

"He's got blinders on."

Hastings sighed. "You're not going to let go, are

you? Find something to pull the blinders off him. You've been around a long time." She scowled, and he laughed. "You have. You know what needs to be done, so do it."

Collins looked into the room and squinted. She took a pad of paper and pen and wrote the names of the seven cases on the wall and turned to her computer. "Hate this thing. Prefer paper. But you gotta do what you gotta do."

Collins entered case file name after case file name, scouring the medical reports for each one.

When she found what she was looking for, she selected a digitized photo or two and sent them to her printer. Then she moved to the next case. When she was finished, she had six photos printed. She grabbed them and headed back into the War Room.

"Hey. Fibbie." She dropped the sheets of paper on Wilson's desk. "Look again."

Wilson took a long look at Collins and handed the pages back to her without looking at them. "Out."

"No. You're going to look at them and you're going to listen to me." She dropped them back on his desk and spread them apart, into three pairs.

She jabbed a finger at the first pair. "From your board. Blower. Nineteen eighty-six. Clear burns from a Taser on his chest. Got a close-up right here for you."

Wilson picked up the close-up and examined it while she talked.

She moved to the next pair. "Schofield. Eighty-one. Tasered in the kidney area. And this one's O'Hara from ninety-three. Zapped in the gut."

Wilson looked at the photos, spreading them out and using a lit magnifier to look at the burn marks. "Well, I can't argue with you. Those burn marks are similar." He stacked the photos and handed them back to Collins. "They didn't exist, Collins. Not before 2000. Definitely not before the mid-nineties. I appreciate the work you've done here, but you're barking up the wrong tree."

Collins held the Blower photo in front of Wilson's face. "So tell me what it is. Anything that makes sense."

Wilson batted the photo away and stood.

Barnes walked in behind Collins with his hands in his pockets. "Let it go, Collins. Back to the cold cases. Let Wilson do his job."

Collins looked at Barnes and shook her head. "Fuck this. Cap, these guys are fucking idiots." She stormed out of the War Room and back to her desk.

Hastings intercepted her. "Take it he wasn't receptive to your suggestions?"

"You must be one of those detectives I've heard so much about." Collins pointed at the War Room. "How do they manage to keep their jobs while being so fucking incompetent?"

Hastings put his hands on her shoulders and gently pushed her down into her chair. "I know what's pissing you off. Freaking out at the FBI isn't going to put Wheeler back behind bars."

"Would it put him six feet under? I'd take that."

He returned to his desk. "Get out of here for a bit. Get some fresh air."

She shook her head and dry scrubbed her face. "Sorry. I've got cold cases to clear. Remember?" She rolled her shoulders. "I'm going to grab another box from the back.

The evidence room sat in the back of the precinct. Collins knocked on the counter and stuck her head in through the hole. "Hey, anybody. Make it snappy."

A young rookie trotted out from behind the shelves. "Sorry detective. Just cleaning things up. What can I do for you?"

Collins checked a name on the piece of paper in her hand. "Case 1986-0032BROOKS." She smiled at the rookie. "You weren't even a gleam in your daddy's eye in 1986, were you? Just buzz me in. I'll grab it."

The cage door buzzed, and Collins pushed in. "Thanks, kid."

She weaved her way to the case file. Hefted the box and smiled. It was a light one. She walked through the stacks and as she rounded a corner knocked another box, labelled "Hopkins, 2003" onto the floor.

"Oh, shit." She placed her case box on the floor and squatted to clean the mess. Files of photos, medical reports and witness statements spilled on the floor with evidence bags and smaller boxes of collected evidence.

She gathered the papers and files together and dropped them in the Hopkins box. Plastic evidence bags went in next. Two boxes remained. She prised the lid off one and looked at the Beretta 92 jammed in it. She put it in the case box and opened the final box. A threaded suppressor was nestled in crumpled paper. She put the lid back on it, tossed it in the spilled case box, and put it back on the shelf.

The young rookie ran back to where she was. "You okay? I heard something drop, but I was busy at the counter."

"I'm fine. Thanks. I appreciate the concern." She hefted the Brook's case file and pushed the rookie out of the way. "I've got it."

He followed her to the cage door.

"Buzz me through, will you kid? My hands are kinda full."

"Yeah, sure. Just don't forget to sign the box out."

Chapter 8

Collins arrived back at her desk with the Brooks file.

"What year's that one from," asked Hastings.

"Eighty-six. You should be in the War Room with all the other super-stars."

Hastings laughed and flipped the folder on his desk shut. "Jealous you're not on it?"

"Relieved. Why aren't you working with them?"

Hastings pointed at his monitor. "Wilson has me looking at the background of all the victims, linking them if possible."

"They were all deadbeats. They all have criminal pasts. They all were shot in the chest," said Collins.

"Or back. Something else, too. Not only did they all have a criminal past, they all—every single one of them—ducked a felony rap just before they were killed."

Collins sat back in her chair. "Huh. A vigilante of some sort."

"Would seem so."

"If we find the perp, we should give him a medal." Collins furrowed her brow in thought. She looked over at Hastings. "Any leads at all who this guy is?"

"Not yet."

"Not even a sniff?"

"Nope. Why?"

Collins scratched at her chin. "Just wondering. Was watching the news last night and it's like they want to rub my face in it. Lead story was Wheeler's release. But they were very thin on details. Have you heard anything?"

"Interesting change of topic."

"He fits your profile."

"Except he's still alive."

"Yeah. Shame, that. So, anything on how he

walked?”

“Like I said, it wasn't anything you did.”

“Yeah, yeah. I need to know how he walked. No defense attorney is that good.”

Hastings put his feet up on his desk. “The prosecution screwed up. Questioned him without an attorney present.”

Collins shook her head. “That's not enough. I caught him in the act. Dead to rights. You were there.”

Hastings scratched the end of his nose. “I really don’t know, Collins.”

“I'm getting a coffee. I seriously can't get my head into this anymore.” She took a deep breath. “I don't think I'm going to last the final month of my career.”

“What are you talking about?”

“Jesus, Hastings. I'm not going to step in front of a bus or anything. Man, you're as melodramatic as a teen girl. Relax a bit.”

Collins grabbed her jacket and walked out of the squad room.

Hastings yelled after her. "Hang on. I could do a coffee."

Chapter 9

The black El Camino rolled to a stop at a meter outside the police station. The driver pulled her tracksuit hood over her head. She took the lanyard with Collins' identification and pass card from her pocket, slipped it around her neck, and got out of the car.

As she walked toward the front of the station Collins left through the front door, hands in her pocket and head down. The Woman paused, smiled and went to enter the station then pulled up.

Hastings walked out after Collins, calling after her. "Hey. Wait up."

The Woman held back and watched as Hastings followed Collins up the street. She waited until they were at least a block away. She grabbed the badge on the end of the lanyard and rubbed it between her thumb and finger.

She walked past the desk sergeant and toward the squad room. She swiped the access card and entered the door into the hectic noise. Nobody paid much attention to her.

She walked with self-assurance to the back of the squad room and to Collins' desk. Papers were strewn across the desktop, a partially disorganized mess. She slid papers and folders around until she found what she was looking for. She grabbed it, opened it to make sure what she was looking for was in it and slid it under her hoodie.

She looked around. Nobody paid attention to her. A crowd gathered in front of the War Room. The Woman had to walk past it to exit. She wandered toward it, stayed behind one of the suits, and listened.

Wilson knocked on the table. "Okay, settle down everybody. I've only got fifteen minutes for this. Settle down." Captain Barnes walked in and stood beside him.

The chatter reduced to a dull roar. Wilson looked around the room at each agent and detective in the task force. His eyes swept past the Woman, and she slid further behind the man in front of her.

"We've got seven related cases. They are linked by both the location they were found and the method of their death. They also are linked in that each of our victims either slipped a felony sentence or were given disproportionately light sentences for serious crimes."

The room was now silent.

"And yes, we've checked. Different lawyers and different judges. It looks like we've got a vigilante on our hands. This is good news for our average law-abiding citizens and not so much for the scum of the earth."

Wilson paused and looked at each member of his task force. "But it doesn't matter if he's a vigilante. We need to stop him."

Barnes stepped forward. "This is basic police work,

people. I recognize for some of you it may be the largest case you've worked on in your career, but it's just basic cop work. Sweat the details."

Wilson nodded. "I want a team looking at all the trace evidence from all of the cases. The killer isn't a genius. Something was left behind. And I want another team looking at ballistics."

The Woman shifted her weight. She slid her hands into her jacket pockets and gripped the file folder she had hidden under it.

Barnes tapped his fingers on the tabletop. "Re-visit the crime scenes. Find out why they were dumped there. Work the trace to find out where they were *actually* killed."

"This isn't rocket science, people," said Wilson. "This is meat and potatoes. It'll get solved with hard, persistent work."

"Wilson won't say it because he's too nice, but fucking pull your heads out of your collective asses and get to work." Barnes pushed past the detectives and FBI agents and left the War Room. The agents and detectives grouped back into their original teams and continued with their work.

The Woman tugged the hood and made a beeline for the exit.

Collins sat at an outside table at the cafe a couple of blocks from the station. A cinnamon roll and a large black coffee sat on the table in front of her. She patted her pockets and extracted a pack of cigarettes. She fished one out, flicked her lighter to life, and a waiter appeared from nowhere.

"No smoking out here."

Collins looked around. "Really? I'm at an outside table."

"Doesn't matter." The waiter pointed at a sign above Collins' head. "City ordinance. And even if it wasn't, we still wouldn't allow it."

Collins snarled at the guy and jammed the cigarette pack back into her pocket. "Fine. Whatever. Leave me alone."

Collins closed her eyes and took a deep breath. The chair across from her rattled. She opened her eyes as Hastings sat.

"Hey, granny," said Hastings. "You okay? You're worrying me."

"Don't you have a serial killer to catch?" she asked, ripping off a piece of cinnamon roll and dunking it in her coffee.

"That's disgusting."

"You haven't tried it." She chewed a bite. "So why wouldn't I be okay?"

"I know you're a tough old bird, but the Wheeler thing, and the rebuff from the FBI, well, that'd piss off anybody."

Collins sipped some coffee and smiled. "I thrive on pissed off. I'm almost always pissed off. Today isn't any different."

Hastings pointed at her coffee cup. "And you drink that swill. How do you have a stomach lining left?"

She took another drink, smiling, holding Hastings' eyes. "I guess I'm just stronger than you, pup." The smile slid off her face, and she sighed. "You're right, though. Wheeler's release has knocked me for a loop. He's going to fuck up and kill more kids, and there's not a damned thing I can do about it."

She ripped off another piece of the roll and chewed. Hastings patiently waited. She finished chewing, swallowed and looked at Hastings. "Oh, Jesus. Harden up a bit, will you? I've been through worse."

Hastings laughed. "That's more like it." He reached for her roll and received a slap on the back of his hand.

"Back off, pup. Get one of your own." She took the last piece of cinnamon roll, washed it down with the last of her coffee and pushed the plate to one side. "Let's go. We've got crimes to solve."

The Woman sat in the black El Camino, flipping through the Wheeler file. She wrote notes on a pad of paper and closed the file. She started to get out of the car, then stopped. Collins and Hastings were walking toward her from the coffee shop.

She slid down in the seat and waited until they entered the police station. She looked at the file she was about to return, then tossed it on the passenger's seat. "Dammit."

Collins hung her jacket on the back of her chair and reopened the box with the Brooks' case file information.

"What ya got?"

"This Brooks guy was found face down in a duck pond some thirty years ago with his throat cut."

"Wife."

Collins shook her head. "Was off in Toronto with her sister at another sister's funeral, so no. Pretty solid alibi. He was an accountant at a small firm downtown. No high profile clients. No known enemies."

"Except the ducks."

Collins frowned. "What?"

"The ducks. He bled in their pond. They *couldn't* be happy about that."

She flipped him the bird. "Dead end. Waste of time. I'm going to have to dig through all these thirty-year-old witness statements, see which ones are still alive and hope like hell they remember something now they didn't then."

"Better you than me. Remind me to never piss off Barnes."

"Brown nose."

"I'm serious. I could never do that. Current cases are hard enough."

"I've got one more after this one. Terry Dunne. Turn of the century." She laughed at the look on his face. "*This* century. 2001." Collins grabbed her phone. "I really can't wait until I retire."

Hastings disappeared into the War Room and the trace team.

"Yeah, see ya, pup. Thanks for the help."

She spent the next two hours trying to track down

anybody who could remember anything about the Brooks murder. Two very fruitless hours. She dropped the handset into the cradle the final time when Hastings made his way back from the task force.

"You look frustrated," said Hastings

"Stop trying to get in my panties, pup. How goes the serial?"

"Better than yours, by the looks of it."

Collins nodded. "This is going back on the shelf. Maybe the Dunne case will bear more fruit."

"That reminds me. I need to pick some fruit up on the way home."

"I'm not touching that with a ten-foot pole." Collins packed the file into the box, popped the lid on it and lifted it to the floor. She lifted some piles of paper off her desk, moved others around.

Hastings grabbed his keys off his desk. "Give it a break. You're working too hard."

"Have you seen the Wheeler file anywhere?"

"You're going to kill yourself over this. Let it go."

"Thanks, Elsa."

Hastings stopped with his coat half on. "Wow. You actually have a cultural reference not from the eighties."

"So, have you seen it? It was on my desk."

Hastings looked at the pile of papers. "If you can find it in that mess you're a better detective than I am. Give it a break. Wheeler's a lost cause. Don't work late. You need your beauty sleep."

"Bitch."

Hastings laughed. "You know it."

Collins watched him leave as she absently pawed through the papers on her desk. "I'm losing it. It was there."

She looked at the Brook case box on the floor and sighed. "What else is there?"

Chapter 10

Collins walked into the evidence room with the Brooks case box in her arms. An older uniform was behind the cage.

"Hey there, Gary. Where's the young guy?"

Gary looked at his watch. "It's seven. We changed shift a while ago. What are you doing here, Collins? Thought you were on the slow slide to irrelevance."

"Fuck you, too. Buzz me in, will you?"

"Just a drop-off?"

"Picking one up, too." She smiled at his frown. "Not going to work it tonight. Just want to be ready when I come in tomorrow. You're worse than my dear departed mother."

Gary pushed a button and the cage door buzzed.

Collins pushed through and nodded. "Got it, Gary. Thanks."

"Need a hand?"

"I'm good." Collins walked past him to the cold case storage area in the back of the room.

Gary turned and watched her walk past. "Maybe when I'm off night shift, we can grab a bite together some night?"

Collins smiled and slowed her walk. She turned, box in hand. "Maybe after I'm out of here, okay? You know, work colleagues and all."

"Yeah, yeah. Sure. Not a bad idea. I'll call you in a couple months, okay?"

"That'd be great." She nodded her head toward the back, toward the cold case file. "Um, I gotta get back to it. Thanks, Gary."

"Sure. Sure."

Collins returned to the task at hand, heading back to the depths of the evidence room. She slid the Brooks box into its space and looked around. "Where are you," she said to herself.

"What ya looking for, Deb?"

Collins jumped. "Jesus, Gary. You scared the hell out of me."

"Sorry 'bout that. Can I help you?"

Collins looked at the Dunne box, on the shelf beside the Hopkins box that she spilled earlier. "I'm good. Thanks."

A bell rang, like a school bell.

"Yeah, there's someone at the counter. Just give me a yell if you need any help."

Collins gave him a two-fingered salute. "You got it."

She waited until he left the area and she could hear him talking to someone at the counter, then pulled the top off the Hopkins box and grabbed the small case holding the Beretta. She lifted the lid on the Dunne box and dropped it in.

She looked back into the Hopkins box at the suppressor, scratched her jaw, and grabbed it, too. She dropped it in the Hopkins box and lifted a couple of file folders from the bottom of the box and covered the gun and suppressor.

"So how's it going?"

"I fucking swear, Gary, if you do that again I'm going to shoot you." Collins took a deep breath and stood. "You're part ninja, right? Didn't hear you walk up behind me twice now." Collins shifted to her left, making sure she blocked his view of the uncovered Hopkins box. "I told you I was okay, didn't I? I'm fine." She placed her hand on his chest. "Don't push too hard, okay? You're a nice guy."

Gary looked down at her and smiled. "Got it. Independent woman. I'm kinda old fashioned. But I guess I can adapt."

Collins winked. "You got it. Let the independent woman do her thing, okay?"

Gary looked at her for a second, then smiled, nodded and turned back the way he came. "I'll be calling you. Don't forget."

Collins squatted down, put the lid back on the Hopkins box and wiped the sweat off her forehead with her sleeve. She hoisted the Dunne box and contemplated what she was about to do.

She walked out of the evidence room with the box in her arms and kicked at the door. "Buzz me, Gary. Hands full."

The door buzzed and she grabbed it with a finger, opening all the way with her foot. "Thanks, Gary."

She adjusted the weight and walked, calm and collected back toward the squad room.

"Hang on, Detective."

Collins stopped. She swore under her breath and turned. "What's up, Gary?"

"That would be Sergeant Davies, Detective." Gary winked. "Gotta keep it professional for a couple more months, right?"

Collins swallowed. "Yeah, right. What is it you called me back for, Sergeant Davies?"

Gary pointed at the logbook. "Gotta sign out."

Collins balanced the box on the shelf and signed out the evidence box. She lifted the box and turned to leave.

"Nuh-uh. Hold up there, Detective."

"What?"

"You didn't sign in the one you brought back."

"Jesus." She repeated the process and signed in the Brooks box.

"Surprised you forgot, Detective. That's a rookie mistake."

Collins nodded and slid the book back across the counter. "A lot on my mind, what with my impending retirement and your, um, advances. Giving me a lot to think about."

"Have a great day, Detective. Don't work too hard, okay?"

Collins smiled and headed back to her desk, arms loaded with her last cold case.

She placed the case box on the floor and looked around. A skeleton crew continued to work in the War

Room. Wilson was still in there as were half a dozen FBI agents and a couple of detectives.

Hastings' desk was empty. A couple of other cops worked late, on the phone or working paperwork, none of them paying attention to her.

She opened her bottom desk drawer and retrieved an ankle holster. She lifted her right pant leg and attached it, then lifted her head and checked.

Still, nobody looking.

She lifted the top off the Dunne box and placed the files on top on her desk. She opened the small case holding the Beretta. She hefted it in her hand, then checked the magazine. Empty, but not a problem. It wasn't difficult acquiring .32 calibre shells.

She slid the Beretta into the ankle holster and dropped her pant leg.

"You're still here?"

She looked up as Captain Barnes walked across the squad room. She dropped the box with the suppressor in her bottom drawer and kicked it shut. She lifted the

Dunne box onto her desk. "You bet. Can't let these cold cases get any colder."

"Go home. It's late." Barnes crossed his arms and stood in front of her desk. "Don't want a fatigue situation."

Collins glanced down at the bottom drawer and back up at Barnes. She flipped one of the files open. "In a few minutes. Just want to tee up some stuff for tomorrow." She read through the file, mentally willing Barnes to leave.

After a moment, he nodded. "I'm out of here. Don't stay late. See you tomorrow."

"Why is everybody so concerned about my well-being? I'll be fine, Captain."

"You know I could take you off the desk, even, for a couple of weeks? Don't over-work it. I'll be checking with the Desk Sergeant tomorrow to make sure you didn't stay late."

"Right. Do that." Collins put her head down and read through the medical examiner's report for Terry

Dunne. Stabbed repeatedly, left in a dumpster and found by a bartender taking out the trash three days after he was killed. The words swam before her eyes.

Out of her peripheral vision she caught Barnes shaking his head and walking away. She waited until he was ascending the stairs to his office until she closed the file.

She pulled the bottom drawer open and took the suppressor out of its box, leaving the box in the drawer. She looked around the squad room, slid the suppressor into her left sock and kicked the drawer shut.

The suppressor shifted and almost fell out. She grabbed at her ankle and managed to keep the suppressor from falling on the floor. She lifted her pant leg and pulled a long strip of clear tape from a dispenser. She wrapped it around her sock and around her leg at the top of the suppressor.

She stood and shook her left leg. It felt secure. At least secure enough to leave the station. She grabbed her jacket and walked out, stopping at the door to the War Room.

"Finally leaving?"

Collins turned and smiled at Barnes, in his jacket and gloves, ready to leave also.

"Finally. How's the serial case going?"

"You wanted on this? It's a dog's breakfast. It's going to take many months to sort all this out. Really slow cycle."

"It's still a hell of a lot more interesting than what I'm doing."

"If you weren't out of here in less than two months, I'd have insisted Wilson put you on this."

"Instead, you insisted he not."

Barnes shrugged. "It's a timing thing. If you had another year in, you'd be on it. Right up front. Smarter cop I've never met."

"Don't worry about it, Cap. See you tomorrow."

Collins walked past the desk sergeant and stopped at the front door to the station. This was it. She had a weapon stolen from the evidence room strapped to her leg. Inside the station, she was still, technically, okay. If she stepped out, though, she was something different. Almost thirty years on the force, and she was always on the right side of it. Sometimes impatient with procedures, but always on the right side of the law.

But it was necessary. She took a deep breath and walked out of the station, contraband handgun strapped to her right leg, illegal silencer on the left. She slid her hands into her pockets. The scrap of paper with Wheeler's address was in there. He wouldn't live the night.

Chapter 11

Collins sat in her car and leaned down to remove the Beretta from her ankle holster. She placed it on the seat beside her and pulled the tape off her left leg, wincing as the tape removed hairs.

"And this is why I don't wax." She threaded the silencer onto the Beretta's muzzle. "Nice balance." She ejected the magazine and looked at its emptiness. "First Walmart, then Wheeler."

Thirty minutes and a $10 stop at Walmart later and Collins rolled to a stop in front of the address in Wheeler's file.

The street light in front of the house was unlit, either a cost-saving measure by the city or, more likely, not maintained. She opened the box of shells and loaded the magazine. She inserted the magazine and racked one into the chamber. She released the mag and added one shell—twelve in the grip and one in the chamber.

She slid the box of ammo under her seat and cracked open the car door. City night noises surrounded her. A domestic squabble in one house tried to overpower the laugh track from a game show in another house. She wasn't sure which sounded more annoying.

A stray dog trotted down the sidewalk. It stopped at the gate to Wheeler's house, cocked a back leg and pissed on the post. Steam rose into the night sky.

"I see you know him," said Collins. The dog looked at her and ran down the street. Collins snugged her jacket around her shoulders and tightened her grip on the gun.

The air was crisp. A plume of condensation left her mouth every time she exhaled. She crunched across the frosty grass and slowly walked up to the rundown bungalow. The lawn was a mess. A couple of old tires sat in the overgrown grass, weeds forcing their way up and through the treads.

She held the Beretta down by her side and eased up the three steps to the front porch. The door was partially open. Most of the house was dark, but she saw a light coming from the back of the house.

She slowly pushed the door open and stepped into the foyer. Something or someone creaked in front of her. She raised the Beretta and padded down the side of the hallway, keeping to the edge of the floor.

A throat cleared in front of her, followed by the noise of someone large sitting in a chair. Cutlery clattered on a table. She gripped the pistol and stepped into the kitchen.

The light above the sink was on, and an elderly Hispanic man sat at the table, eating a sandwich. He saluted her with his bottle of beer.

She tightened her grip. "Detective Collins. Who are you?"

"I take it you're looking for Wheeler." He took another bite of his sandwich and chased it with a mouthful of beer. "

"I said who are you?"

"Jorge Castillo, Detective. You can put the gun down."

Collins stepped closer, Beretta not wavering. "What are you doing here? Do you live with Wheeler? Where is he?"

"Ha. I'm a neighbor. The scumbag left early this afternoon. Took a bunch of bags with him. Didn't look like he was coming back." He held up his sandwich. "Guy buys a great cut of meat. Thought I'd help myself. Have a seat, Detective."

Collins pulled out a chair and sat, gun still trained on Jorge.

"Look, Detective, I'd appreciate it if you pointed your weapon somewhere else. This is a good sandwich. But I don't want to die for it."

Collins placed the gun on the table in front of her.

"He left this afternoon?"

"A bit after lunch." He took another bite from his sandwich. "And a good lunch it must have been." He nodded at the Beretta. "That doesn't look much like a cop gun."

"About that."

"Hey, don't let me pry. I don't care. You want to shoot Wheeler, I sure as hell ain't gonna stop you. Just promise me you shoot his nuts off first." Jorge took a pull on his beer and suppressed a belch. "Excuse me."

He put the bottle down on the table and leaned forward, eyes squinted, looking closely at Collins. "So tell me, Detective, how in the hell did that slimy piece of shit walk? I thought it was a solid case, what I read in the papers."

"Do you know where he went?"

"We didn't socialize much, what with his propensity for kiddies. I shoulda cut his nuts off years ago."

"You knew what he was?"

"Knew is a strong word, but we had ideas what kind

of person he was."

"We?"

"A lot of the guys in the neighborhood." He shook his head. "If I knew how bad it was, he'd be dead right now." Jorge nodded at the Beretta. "That's what you're doing, right?"

Collins picked the Beretta off the table and unscrewed the suppressor. The cylinder dropped into her jacket pocket, and the Beretta slid into her ankle holster. "What can you tell me about him? His haunts, where he works, what he drives."

"We didn't play poker together. We sure as hell didn't exchange recipes. All I know is he barreled out of here with a couple of Hefty bags, tossed them in his puke green Corolla and fucked off in a cloud of smoke. And good riddance to him."

Collins sat back in the chair. "About eight hours ago."

"Yeah, that's about right. Sorry. Hey, can I go with you? I want a shot at him."

"He hurt someone you know?"

"He hurts kids, Detective. That's enough reason." Jorge emptied the bottle and belched. "There was a guy. Something or other Watkins. He'd come by every once in a while."

"First name?"

"Something or other. Thought I already told you." He laughed. "No idea. A good foot shorter than Wheeler, close-cropped greasy hair and a gut that tested the tensile strength of his T-shirt."

Collins laughed. "Should be easy to identify." She stood and pushed her chair into the table. "Eight hours ago."

"Thereabouts."

"Fuck."

"Exactly."

"Nice meeting you, Jorge. If you run into this guy, feel free to kick him in the nuts as hard as you can."

Jorge laughed and stood with her. "Will do, Detective. I suppose I should leave. Don't want to get arrested for trespassing."

"I'm homicide. Trespass all you want. Any other food, or beer, you want to take, feel free."

"Detective. I'm shocked." Jorge smiled and opened the fridge. He grabbed the remaining beer. "Ate the food already. The good stuff, anyway. You alone? Need anyone to ride shotgun?"

"You hitting on me? I've got a gun, remember?"

Jorge held up his hands, most of a six-pack in one of them. "Nope, I'm not hitting on you. Wouldn't think of it. You got a number I can call if he shows up?"

Collins pulled a card out of her wallet and handed it to him. "Call my cell if you see him. Or his buddy. Okay?"

Jorge looked at the card, smiled and slipped it his pack pocket. "You got it. I'm not going to bother locking the house up, if that's okay with you."

"Fine. I've got work to do. Stay out of trouble."

"Always, Detective."

Collins walked out of the house, hands in her

pocket, deep in thought. "He's running. Shit. Not as stupid as I thought he was."

Chapter 12

Collins parked in front of a line of Harleys, blocking them in. She checked the Beretta in her ankle holster and stepped out of the car. A thickset bald man, wearing sunglasses at 10:00 at night stood at the door to the club.

"Detective."

"Good evening, Julio. I'm going in."

"Can't stop ya."

"Nope. Everything cool in there? I'm not looking to bust anyone, unless the guy I'm looking for is in there."

"Nothing extremely illegal happening. Who you gunning for?"

Collins pulled the club door open. "That pedo fuck

Wheeler."

"Wouldn't let him in. Go ahead, ask all you want."

The door closed behind Collins. She stood in the smoky bar and inhaled. There was weed mixed in with the smoke, but she didn't care. The smell of stale beer almost overpowered the smell of pot anyway.

Southern rock blasted from the speakers, drowning out any conversation unless you had your mouth to an ear.

She pushed between a couple of greasy leathers and leaned on the bar, waving the bartender over.

The man on the left of her grabbed her ass. "Hey, blondie. Tight ass for an old bird."

She reached back, grabbed his hand and twisted his arm hard enough to slam his face into the bar. "Old enough to be your mother, you punk." She gave the arm an extra twist and let him go.

His friends laughed. The fat one on the other side of her dropped his beer he was laughing so hard. "Holy fuck. She's half your size, man. Jesus."

Collins ignored him and pointed at a photo of Wheeler on her phone. "I'm looking for this guy. You seen him around anywhere?"

The bartender took the phone and squinted at it. "The asshole who got off, right? The pedo."

"I didn't ask you to identify him. I know who in the hell he is. Has he been in here?"

The bartender shook his head. "Never. He wouldn't last a minute in here, anyway."

Collins took the phone back. "Thanks." She dropped her card on the bar. "If he *does* show up, call me. And don't kill him all the way before I get here."

She stepped over the broken bottle and left the bar. Julio held the door for her. "Thanks."

"You find who you were looking for, Detective?"

"Not yet." She opened her car door. "But I will."

The Woman followed Collins when she left the bar and tailed her to her apartment. She had to struggle to keep up in places. Collins ran a couple of stale yellow lights and a red on her way home.

Which she reached in record time. The Woman parked half a block away and settled in for a wait.

Collins entered her apartment and slammed the door shut. "Son of a bitch. Where are you?" She hung her jacket on a tree. She dropped her service revolver and shield in a wooden bowl by the front door.

She removed the ankle holster and looked at it and the Beretta for a second. Then she opened her closet, tipped a pair of seldom worn pumps out of their box, dropped the Beretta and suppressor in it and slid the box onto the top shelf.

She blew out a breath and stuck her head in the refrigerator. She grabbed a couple of slices of old pizza and a can of beer. She made her way to the living room, dropped into her recliner and turned on the TV. The news, with an update on the Wheeler release, came up first.

"Oh, for fuck's sake."

She changed the channel to a re-run of a police procedural. She took a long pull of beer, muted the television and scrolled through the numbers on her phone.

Most of her contacts she'd already called. There was one, though, who she couldn't reach. She poked the green button.

After a couple of rings the person on the other end picked up.

"Geezer, that you?"

Geezer was a tall, lanky kid in his early twenties. The raucous sounds of strip club music played in the background, unenthusiastic strippers performing on a small stage for an even smaller crowd.

"Who else would it be?"

"Where are you?"

"Work." Geezer pressed the phone to his head, finger in the opposite ear.

"Since when did you have a job?"

"What do you want, Detective?" Geezer looked over his shoulder and walked toward the door. "You shouldn't be calling me here."

"And how would I know you were there when I didn't even know you had a job? I'm not in the mood for this. I'm looking for Wheeler. Keep an eye open for me."

The Woman in the El Camino wiped condensation off the inside of the windows. She cranked up the heat and rolled down the driver's side window. The cold air was bracing. She put on a pair of headphones and picked up a parabolic microphone. She pointed it out the window at Collins' apartment building. Silence, at first, then she panned it a bit to the left and picked up Collins' voice on the phone.

"Fuck off, Geez. Tell your friends. A c-note for the first person to tell me where I can find him. Text me any time, day or night."

Silence for a minute, then:

"Believe it or not, Geez. First person to lead me to that scum gets the money."

The Woman dropped the parabolic mic on the passenger's seat, on top of the Wheeler file. She took off the headphones and rolled up the window. "Stay there for a few hours, Detective. Don't want you interrupting me."

Collins dropped her phone on the table beside her chair and unmuted the television. One of the many variations of a familiar cop show rolled credits and a bump came on promoting a show filled with talking heads debating current pedophile laws. Wheeler was used as an example.

"Fucking hell!" She grabbed an ashtray off the table and threw, shattering it against the wall beside her plasma television. "Dammit."

A voice on the other side of the wall filtered through. "We're trying to sleep over here. Shut up or I'll call the cops."

Collins put her face close to the wall. "I *am* a cop. *You* shut up, or I'll come over and have a chat with you face to face."

She finished the beer and turned off the TV. She was retrieving a broom and dustpan from under her sink when her phone rang.

She looked at the display and shook her head. "What is it Hastings? How did you know I wasn't already tucked in bed?"

Hastings laughed. "Your age? You probably only sleep four or five hours a night. Just calling to make sure you're okay. Was a rough day today."

Collins returned to her chair. She looked at the shattered glass on the floor and tossed the cleaning equipment in its general direction. "I've had worse. Don't baby me."

"I wouldn't. But I do worry about you, especially after Wheeler's release."

"I should have killed him when I caught him. Save us all a lot of grief. And money." She shook the beer can and scowled at its emptiness. "Is that the only reason you called?"

"No. Looking at a different angle on the serial case. Wanted to bounce some things off you."

Collins levered herself out of her chair. "I'm going to need another beer for this. What's the theory?" She took another can from the fridge and sat back in her chair. "Yeti killed them?"

"We've got this fantastic lake right by the city."

"I know. The wind coming off it today damned near froze my tits off. What about it?"

"Why haven't the bodies been dumped there? Why out in the open where, first of all, they'd be found almost immediately and, more importantly, would be almost impossible to dump without being noticed."

"Yet, they did. Dump them undetected, I mean." She popped the top on the can. "So what are you thinking? You wouldn't call me without an idea."

"Clearly, the perp wanted the victims to be found."

"Vigilantes usually do. Anything else?"

"Partially. I think the perpetrator has a link to law enforcement. Cleaning up the messes the courts make. And putting the cleaned up mess where everyone could see them."

Collins nodded. Realised Hastings couldn't see her and cleared her throat. "That's good theory. Have you shared it with Wilson? You should. It would focus their investigation."

"I will be tomorrow. Wanted to bounce it off you first."

"No you didn't. You just wanted to include me. And I really appreciate it, Hastings. I do. Now piss off and let me watch Monk reruns."

Hastings chuckled, gravel in a coffee can across the phone lines. "You know me too well. See you tomorrow."

Collins hung up and tossed her phone on the table beside her. She leaned back and closed her eyes. In a few minutes, she was asleep.

Chapter 13

The Woman parked her El Camino in the same spot she had parked it the day before. She slid the Wheeler file under her jacket, pulled the hood up for concealment and put on a pair of large sunglasses. She exited the car, striding confidently to the squad room. She gave the War Room a wide berth and walked to Collins' desk.

She pulled the file from under her jacket and put it on the desk. She thought for a moment, then wrote a quick note and slid it into the file.

She nudged the Dunne cold case file with her foot, cocked her head as she looked at it, then lifted it onto the desk. She flipped off the top and pulled out the case file, and sat back in the chair.

"Stabbed repeatedly, left in a dumpster and found by a bartender taking out the trash." She flipped to the crime scene photos. "Not one of mine." She spread the crime scene photos across the desk.

Blood pooled in the bottom of the dumpster, clearly emptied just prior to the crime. The photos showed a middle-aged man, in an expensive suit and shoes, gone to pot and covered in blood. A trail of blood drops started in the middle of the alleyway and tracked to the dumpster.

She checked the medical examiner's report. Defensive wounds on the hands and forearms indicated resistance. Personal effects included a wallet with cash and a couple of credit cards, a jade signet ring and Phillip Patek watch. She smiled. "I remember this one." She scribbled another note and placed it in the medical file.

Wilson walked up while she was putting the lid on the box and the box on the floor. "Excuse me. This is Detective Collins' desk, isn't it?"

The Woman looked up from under her hood. "I believe so. Why?"

"What are you doing here?"

"I'm from the 3rd. Collins wanted some background info on a cold case she's working on. A Terry Dunne. Case from 2001. She thinks it might be mob-related, and I've done some work with your colleagues in the Organized Crime Taskforce." She looked at her watch. "Hey, gotta run." She took out her phone and started dialing. "I'll give her a call and let her know I was here. Thought she might be working late."

She pushed past Wilson and stopped at the War Room.

Wilson followed and stood behind her. "Who in Organized Crime? You look familiar."

"You probably don't know them. They're out of Jersey, and it was thirteen, fourteen years ago." She pointed at the crime board. "What's this?"

"Surprised you haven't heard. Collins was going through a bunch of cold cases and found four linked to a current murder. A little more digging found two more."

The Woman looked at the names on the board. All names she knew. All killings she had made. "Collins put it together, did she?"

"Yup. Too bad she's retiring. Her captain asked me to keep her off the task force. Could use her kind of out-of-the-box thinking."

"Right." The Woman slid the sunglasses down her nose and ran her fingers over the names, recalling each and every one of them. "So how's it going?"

Wilson shrugged. "It's not a normal serial case. The duration between kills varies and in some cases it's years. We're working against a clock, but we don't know how fast it's ticking. There are patterns in the kills and the dump sites, but there's so much we don't know."

"It's all leg work. Patient, time-consuming leg work."

Wilson nodded. "But I have a gut feeling we don't

have time."

The Woman pointed at one of the pictures. "This?"

"Yeah, well, those are burns that we found on four of the seven bodies. Collins seems to think they're Taser burns."

"Really?"

"I know, right? Tasered in the eighties? I don't know what they are, but they're common to four of them. Anyway." Wilson pulled his coat off a hanger. "You're going to have to leave. I'm out of here and I don't want anyone in here unsupervised."

"Yeah. Sure." The Woman read down a list of actions on the board. "Zeroing in on the location from the dump sites? I would have thought locating the kill sites would be a better idea."

"I've got a team looking at trace on the bodies to try to find the place they were killed, but we're not getting far. Ballistics results will be back in a day or so. That may show something." He jerked his thumb toward the door. "You gotta go."

The Woman slid the sunglasses back up, shoved her hands in her pockets and walked past the FBI Agent. "Thanks."

She walked out of the station and into the parking lot. A cold wind blew off the lake, promising snow. She pulled off her sunglasses, hunched her neck into her jacket, unlocked the car and jumped in.

She sat there for a minute while the engine warmed up. "Ballistics. Shit."

Chapter 14

Collins' phone rang and she slowly came awake in the recliner. She looked around, trying to get her brain up to speed. She forced her eyes open wide and looked at the phone. Through the blears, she saw Hastings' name on the screen.

And the time. It was 9:30.

"Yeah. Hastings. What's up?"

"Where are you? How late were you working?"

Collins groaned and lifted herself out of the chair, wincing and grabbing at her lower back. "Overslept. I'll be there in an hour or so. If anyone's looking for me, I'm talking to a CI about something, okay?"

"Take the day, maybe. Call in sick."

Collins opened the fridge and shook the orange

juice carton. "But I'm not. See you in an hour."

She tipped the carton back and drained the orange juice, ran her tongue over her teeth, grimaced, and headed to the bathroom.

Almost exactly an hour later Collins walked in through the squad room, tapping on Hastings desk as she passed it. "Anybody looking for me?"

"You're good. What happened?"

"I'm old. Up late yelling at my neighbour through the wall and fell asleep in front of the TV."

"Drinking again?"

"Two lite beer. Nothing. Much as I hate to admit it, it's probably the stress about Wheeler walking." She exhaled a breath. "Anywho, I've got a cold case to crack."

"What a lightweight. Two beer. What'll the rest of the guys think?"

"Shove it, pup." Collins draped her jacket over the back of her chair and headed to the coffee machine.

"Can I get you one?"

"Three already today, granny. None for me."

She poured a large cup of black coffee and returned to her desk.

"Are you hung-over? Seriously?"

"Two lite beers? You're kidding, right?" She sat and absent-mindedly shuffled papers on her desk. She picked up the Wheeler file and was putting it to one side when she realized what she had in her hand.

She opened it and the lanyard with her identification card slid out. "Did you put this here?"

"What?"

She waved the lanyard. "This. On my desk. In the Wheeler file I *know* wasn't there yesterday."

"Ri-i-i-ight."

"I'm not going senile. If you didn't do it, who did?"

"It was under a piece of paper or something. Who cares?"

"Someone's been messing with my desk." She put the lanyard around her neck and strode toward the

War Room.

"Don't go picking a fight you can't win," Hastings yelled after her.

Collins targeted Wilson and pulled him into a corner. "Have you had one of your minions messing around on my desk?"

"What in the hell are you talking about, Detective-" he looked down at her lanyard, "-Collins?"

"Papers are coming and going on my desk. I'm not quite old enough for mad cow, and none of *my* colleagues are fucking with me. They wouldn't dare."

"None of the task force would have any reason to look at anything on your desk. You're imagining things. Retiring soon, right?"

Collins crossed her arms. "I want you to ask each and every one of your team, individually, if they've been at my desk."

Wilson shook his head. "I'm not. It was probably your friend from the 3rd."

"Who?"

"She was in here last night. At your desk." He registered the blank look on her face. "You don't know? She said she was helping you with some cold cases. Can't remember the name. Said it was mob related and she was checking her contacts." He stood. "You really don't know, do you?" He started walking out of the War Room. "This is your desk right?" He pointed at it as he walked toward it. "In the corner?"

"Yeah. Describe him."

"Her."

"Describe *her*? I don't know any female detectives in the Third."

Wilson shrugged. "Short, thinner than you. Short dark hair. Didn't really get a good look at her. Wore sunglasses. Inside." He shook his head. "Didn't think I'd have to pick her out of a line-up."

Collins looked at her desk in a new light. "Jesus. Do I have to get the techs up here?" She sat at her desk. "You didn't get her name?"

"She was walking around like she owned the place.

No, I didn't get her name."

Collins picked up her phone. "That's horseshit. The Third?"

"I'll make a call too. She said she had worked with the Organized Crime team out of Jersey a dozen years ago."

"No, I'll call them. I've got some contacts there too, from the nineties and my misbegotten youth. You've got a serial killer to find."

Wilson cocked his head. "Who'd you work with?"

Collins stopped in mid-dial. "Oh, what's his name? Ended up in Miami a few years ago, the schmuck. But he'd know her. Steven James. Steve-o, I called him. He hated it. Working a liaison gig with Miami PD now. Still a Fed."

Wilson shook his head. "Okay. I don't know him. Let me know if you need any help with this. Check your stuff. Make sure nothing is missing."

"You think? Let me call my friend at the Third."

Collins finished dialing and tuned Wilson out.

After a couple of rings a familiar voice answered. "Detective Peterson."

"Collins here. You got a minute?"

"Cock-block Collins. As I live and breathe."

Collins barked a laugh. "*I* cock-blocked *you*? Give me a break. How's things?"

"Fair to middling. What you callin' about?"

"Can't a friend call and say hi?"

"You haven't in the six years since you left. You want something."

Collins chewed the inside of her lip. "Yeah. Someone was messing around at my desk last night, while I was gone. Told someone she was from the Third helping me with a cold case I'm working on. I don't have anybody from your shop helping me. Trying to track her down."

"If she lied about helping you, she probably lied about being from the Third."

"Whatever. You got a jockey-sized brunette female detective there?"

There was a pause. "Nah. The only lady-type detectives here are Saginovski, and she's almost six foot, and Milligan, the round red-head. Doesn't ring a bell. When you up here again? You owe me a beer."

"One of these days. Look, I've gotta go. Keep an ear open for me, okay?"

"You got it."

Collins hung up and scrolled through the numbers on her phone until she found the one she was looking for. She called from her mobile.

"Special Agent Steven James speaking."

"Steve-o."

"Well. Detective Collins. What can I do for you? I thought you were out of the mob stuff. Chasing pedophiles, or some such thing."

Collins smiled. "We don't like each other, Steve. Fine. But I need to check something with you. Someone rifled through my desk last night and she told the person who interrupted her she was helping me with a cold case, with mob ties, and she'd worked with the Jersey office thirteen, fourteen years ago. You were there, then, right?"

"Yeah. What's his name?"

"You're not paying attention, Steve-o. 'She'. And if I knew her name, I wouldn't be calling you. Short, slight dark-haired she-detective out of Detroit. Says she's from the Third. Ring any bells?"

"Only you, and you're a blondie. No. Nothing. Good luck tracking them down. Now, ah, if you'll excuse me, I'm trying to tail a suspect in a large gambling thing that's going down. If you're ever in Miami, don't look me up."

He hung up, and Collins looked at her phone. "What a twat."

Hastings stood by her desk. "No luck, I take it."

Collins sat back in her chair and ran her fingers through her hair. "Annoying. But nothing." She grabbed the Wheeler file. "What the hell was she looking for?"

Hastings walked back to his desk. "Hey, if you want

me to help out with anything, I'm here."

"Thanks." She opened the Wheeler file and flipped through the pages. A piece of paper under the ME's report slipped out onto her desk. She slowly put the Wheeler file to one side and picked up the note. "Hey, dickweed, is this your idea of a joke?"

"What now?"

She read from the note. *"Now look what you've done. Retire, why don't you?"*

"What the hell is that supposed to mean?"

Collins crumpled it, tossed it in the trash, and put the Wheeler file to one side. "I don't even know if it was meant for me. Maybe it's been in there all along, and I didn't notice it."

She stood and hoisted the Dunne file box onto her desk and removed the top. "Last one, Hastings." She dropped the lid on the desk and pulled out the ME file. "Stabbed." She sat as she opened it. Another sheet of paper fell out.

"Fucking hell." She read the note and sat back in

her chair. Then she turned her attention to the ME's report.

"What now?"

"Hang on a second." She took the evidence photos and spread them out on her desk and started comparing the pictures with both the ME report and the note left in the file.

"Well, hell."

"You gonna tell me?"

"So whoever this was here last night might have actually cleared the Dunne case for me."

Hastings dropped hat he was working and came to her desk. "You got a guardian angel?"

Collins handed him the ME file. "Chubby middle-aged dude stabbed and dumpstered. Not a robbery, 'cause he's got a shitload of bling on him." She held up a note. "According to my mystery guest, Dunne was an accountant for the Morales crime family who was skimming and was punished. I'll give Steve a call later and confirm, but I've got vague memories of

Morales, and this is something he'd have done."

"So pick up Morales and sweat him."

Collins smiled. "Youngsters. He was knocked off by a competing family a few years ago. Big headlines. Surprised you don't remember."

"Enough crime to keep me busy without poking my nose into the Family business."

She piled the photos and the ME report and dropped them back in the box. "I've got to call Steve James back, and I hate talking to him. I'm going to need a breath of fresh air first." She grabbed her jacket and a pack of cigarettes. "What are you looking at?"

"Fresh air?"

"*My* lungs. None of *your* business. I'll be back in a few."

"Bad habit."

She pulled on her jacket. "My habit."

Chapter 15

The wind off the lake amplified the cold, and Collins hunched into her jacket in an attempt to keep warm. "The things I do for a smoke." She cupped her hands around her lighter to protect the flame from the wind and inhaled. She pocketed her lighter and exhaled with a smile on her face. "Ah. That's better."

She walked around the corner to a laneway between buildings to get out of the wind and away from the pervasive 'No Smoking' signs. She took another drag and turned her back to the wind.

As she exhaled, a hand pushed her in the center of her back, between the shoulder blades, and pressed her face into the wall. Her cigarette broke and fell to the ground.

"Fucking hell, do you know who I am?" She tried to turn to face her attacker and was met with a silencer jammed in her neck.

The Woman leaned forward and whispered in her ear. "Shh."

Collins stopped and held her hands out to her sides. "Take it easy. There's CCTV out here. You kill me, and you won't see the sun set."

"I'm not going to kill you," the Woman whispered.

"What was that?"

The Woman cleared her throat and spoke quietly. "I know who you are. You've got a problem."

Collins started to turn and the Woman pushed the silencer hard under her jaw. "Hey. *I* have a problem? Not from my side of the table. You are being extremely stupid."

The Woman chuckled quietly. "You've been busy. Was the Taser thing you? It seems like it's something you would pick up." She gave Collins a nudge with the silencer. "You'd be smart to convince them you were wrong."

"I've got nothing to do with that case."

"You triggered it. I saw those names on the board." The Woman paused. "You've been around. I'd like to think you've got some influence."

Collins burst out laughing. "Oh, you've really got the wrong lady. I'm being put out to pasture. I'm stuck with cold cases until I retire. Saggy old tits, I am." She turned her head into the silencer. "Did you write in Dunne's case file? Mob-related hit?"

"Look into it. You'll find I'm right."

Collins slowly lowered her right hand to her service revolver and got a jab in the neck for her troubles.

"No, no. Both hands up."

Collins slowly raised her hands well above her head. "So what's your end game? We going to stand out here all fucking day? It's cold."

"I noticed. Would rather be in Florida."

"Too humid. Phoenix, maybe."

"Maybe." The Woman leaned closer. "If the serial

case progresses much further-"

Collins turned hard to her right, her arms still up, and caught the Woman on the side of the head.

As the Woman fell, Collins pulled out her revolver and levelled it at her assailant. The Woman had a jacket on, the hood over her head. She pushed herself up on to her hands and knees and collected her gun. "That wasn't nice."

"On your knees, hands behind your head and interlace your fingers."

The Woman stayed on her hands and knees, back to Collins. "How did you tie the cases together?"

"I said hands behind your head."

"I heard what you said. I asked you a question."

Collins lowered the gun slightly. "It's been you who's been doing these killings, hasn't it?"

The Woman rolled back onto her knees, her hands out to her sides and her back to Collins. She shrugged. "Anyone on that list you think I should have spared?" She slowly stood.

"On your knees!"

"I don't think so." She kept her back to Collins and slowly lowered her arms. "You looked at those cases. Each of them. You know who those," she paused, "people are. Tell me it wasn't the right thing to do." She rolled the cuffs down on her sleeves. "It is cold out here. You're right. Phoenix doesn't sound too bad."

"You actually expect me to let you walk, don't you?"

"Detective Collins, I *am* going to walk. And you're going to do whatever you can to sideline the FBI."

"Who are you?"

The Woman started walking away. "You'll find out one day, but it won't matter by then." She yelled back as she left the alley. "Remember what I said. Shut down that serial case any way you can. At the very least, give it a very wide berth."

Collins lowered her revolver as the Woman walked away. "What the fuck?"

Hastings ran up behind her, his service revolver drawn. "What in the hell are you doing?"

"Where'd you come from?"

"I saw it on the CCTV." Hastings continued past Collins, revolver at his side. He poked his head around the corner, holstered his gun and walked back to Collins. "What the hell, Collins? You going senile? You let him go."

"Her. Why were you watching CCTV?"

"It's a damned good thing I was. Her? That was a woman?"

Collins looked at the cigarette on the ground, sighed and lit a new one. "Kinda small for a man, right?" She took a long drag. "I don't know what it was about. You didn't answer me. Why were you watching the video?"

"I do sometimes. Run through all of them. Someone has to. I'm glad I did." He took her by the arm. "We've got to go report this."

Collins pulled her arm free. "It was nothing."

"She had a gun on you. Nothing?"

"It wasn't loaded. I guess. Look, I want to look into this myself first. She didn't harm me, and she's the one who was digging around on my desk. I'm going to do a little bit of quiet investigation on my own."

Hastings looked up at the cameras in the alley. He pointed to the far end. "I got vision from that one, but," He pointed at the one above them, "nothing from that one."

"Figures." She ground the cigarette out under her toe. "I'm going back in. Thanks for the support. Even if it wasn't necessary."

The Woman got around the corner at a walk, then broke into a sprint. She ran across the street against traffic and jumped into the El Camino and started the engine. She let out a long slow breath and shook her head. "That was stupid. Jesus, what was I thinking?" She punched at the steering wheel and pulled from the curb. "Get a grip. It's almost finished. Almost."

Chapter 16

Hastings grabbed Collins by the arm and spun her around. "You tell me what in the hell is going on, Collins. What are you sitting on?"

Collins wrenched free, shoved him against the wall and pressed her hand against his chest. "What am I sitting on? I'm clearing out cold cases. Maybe that bitch is afraid I'm getting too close to something."

He pushed her hand away. "You've been at this precinct eight years and in that eight years you've been the hardest piece of work. Twice you had complaints filed for excessive force."

"Three times."

"Fine. And I just watched you let someone who had a piece jammed in your neck walk away like nothing happened." He looked down on Collins. "So tell me what it was about."

Collins held his gaze for a minute then looked away. "I don't know. Honestly do not know." She put her head down and her hands in her pockets. "There's something very strange happening and I can't get my head around it."

"So fucking talk about it. I'm not as dumb as I look."

Collins cracked a half smile. "Hard to believe." She shook her head and started walking to the front of the station, Hastings beside her.

"Talk, Collins."

"I don't know." She hesitated. "I don't know how to explain it. This person, if it was the same one, left enough information in the Dunne file to effectively close it." She shrugged. "I would have closed it eventually, but maybe not all of it before I left." She held the door for Hastings. "So, a helpful asshole. Then today, she sticks me in the neck and tells me it would be smart if I tried to shut down the serial case."

"*The* serial case?" Hastings laughed. "She thought you have that kind of kick over the FBI?"

"I know. Nuts, right?" She blew out a breath. "So I'm going to grab the vision from outside and see what I can see."

She sat at her desk and accessed the video feeds from the cameras around the station.

"I'll put a car outside your apartment building." Hastings picked up his phone a poked a couple of buttons.

"Oh, hell no. Put that down. The half-wit thought I could tank the serial case. She clearly doesn't know me. She sure as hell doesn't know where I live."

Hastings slowly lowered the receiver. "You sure?"

"What did I just say?" She returned her attention to the video. "Which cameras cover the alley?"

"I was looking at W27. So that one and E27."

Collins nodded and clicked through to the log files. "Shit."

"What?"

"E27's dead. Most recent file is from over two months ago. Jesus. Doesn't anyone take care of this shit?" She opened the window for W27 and scrubbed it back thirty minutes. "There's a zoom on this, right?"

"Press 'control' and the plus sign and the same time."

Collins blew the image up until it fill her monitor. She stepped it forward frame-by-frame until she got to the point the gun was jammed in her neck. "Shit." She leaned forward, squinting. "Useless."

Hastings left his desk and sat beside her. "She's got that hood almost completely over her head."

"Yeah." Collins pushed her chair back. "Wait here."

She trotted into the War Room and found Wilson. "You got a minute?"

"Not really. Kinda busy."

"I know. I've got vision of someone. Want you to tell me if it's the person who was at my desk last night."

"Certainly. Gimme a sec. I'll be right there."

Collins made her way back to her desk. Hastings was manipulating something on the screen. "What do you have?"

He rolled to one side and made room for her. "I grabbed the shot and cropped out everything but her head. And tried to enhance it." He looked over at the War Room where Wilson had left his desk and was on his way over. "Cropped out the gun in the neck, too."

Collins raised an eyebrow. "Thanks. It doesn't show much more, though. Just a sliver of her face."

"Yeah. She's white and she's got dark hair. That could be anybody."

"We're in Detroit, Hastings, not as many as if we were in Seattle."

"Don't go all racist on me, granny."

Wilson walked up to her desk. "What do you have?"

Collins spun her monitor around so he could see it. "Recognize her?"

Wilson leaned forward and squinted at the screen. "This is it?" He stood and smiled at Collins. "A grainy side shot of someone in a hood, with no height or weight reference? All you got is the tip of her nose and a bit of hair. Useless."

"So you're saying you can't tell if this is the same person, Wilson?"

The FBI Agent looked at Collins through slitted eyes. "She had one of those hoods on, and the hair may have been the same color, but that's not enough to make a positive identification.

"Just asking. Thanks. As you were."

"Wasting my time like that is a bad idea, Collins. Hastings, you should know better." He turned and strode back into the War Room.

Collins watched him walk away. "He was no help."

Hastings nodded and moved his chair back to his desk. "He's focused on something else. You've got to decide what you're going to do."

"Nothing." She closed the video windows and lifted the Dunne box onto her desk. "I've to finish her work here." She opened the medical examiner's file and took out the note and placed it on her desk. She scrolled through her phone and found the number she was looking for and dialed it on her desk phone.

"Special Agent James speaking."

"Steve-o. Your balls still sweaty?"

"Jesus, Collins. What do you want?"

Collins pulled the ME report closer. "You ever have anything to do with the Morales family?"

"Once upon a time. They were up your way. Fell apart about a decade or so ago. Why?"

"Who ran their numbers?" Collins held up the picture of Dunne in the dumpster. "Fat fuck named-"

"Terry Dunne. Disappeared while we were cracking down on the family. He was supposed to testify at the trial. Fortunately, we had his books and a good prosecuting attorney. Didn't bother looking for him that hard. We were focused more on the main man. Why you bringing this old shit up now?"

"We're trying to clear the Dunne case. Some cafe shop worker found his body in a dumpster a couple of days after he was killed. Multiple stab wounds. Must have been a long blade to get through that fat."

"Was there anything missing?"

Collins took the phone from her head and looked at it. "What?"

"Any part of his body missing? Cut off, maybe."

Collins quickly scanned through the autopsy report. On the third page she found what he was talking about. "There was a chunk taken out of his hide. The ME estimated it was-"

"A pound of flesh. Yeah. That makes sense."

"Makes sense? What in the fuck makes sense about that?" Collins tossed the file on to her desk.

"There's a killer for hire. Or there was. He's dead. I killed him. Killed him good. Nasty fucker named Sajok. Really liked knife work. The messier the better. You won't find any evidence on the body to tie it to him."

Collins wrote notes on the file. "Sajok?"

"George Sajok. Look him up. Put aside a day. The

file is large. It's all moot now, Collins. Morales is dead, the guy he hired to kill Dunne is dead and Dunne is dead. You can close them all. Now if you'll excuse me, Detective, I've got to run."

She dropped the handset into the cradle and tossed the file into the box. "Done."

"Was she right?"

"Who, the hooded marvel? Yeah. She was right. Didn't name the killer, but she got the rest of it."

"How?"

Collins looked at Hastings. "That's an excellent question. The FBI had Dunne on a leash, then he disappeared. He was supposed to testify and didn't, so you'd think that if they didn't know what happened to him, nobody did."

"But she did."

"Like you said, 'how'." Collins laced her fingers behind her head, leaned back and looked at the ceiling. "Who *is* that bitch?"

"Hey, I gotta go. Barnes is coming down the stairs.

Another briefing for the cool guys, I think."

Collins sat up as her phone beeped. She looked at the message. "Yeah, okay. CI just messaged me. I've got to take this outside."

"Be careful."

"If she wanted me dead, I'd be dead." Collins grabbed her jacket and stuffed her phone in her pocket. "Let me know what the feds are talking about when you get back, okay?"

"If you're still alive. Sure."

Chapter 17

Collins walked out of the station and around to the back. She took a quick look in both directions and pushed her back up against the wall. Nobody would sneak up on her this time.

She took another quick look around and read the message: *"I think I got something. Call me."* From Geezer. Of all the CIs she had, the dumbest one came through. "Hallelujah."

She called him.

"Who's this?"

"Geez, I'm hurt. You don't have me in your phone? Got your message."

"Oh yeah. Collins."

She closed her eyes and leaned her head against the

brick wall. "You stoned, Geez?"

"Had a bit of bud. Why, you a narc now?"

Collins sighed and folded an arm across her chest. "Spit it out."

"So I heard that the pedo and his buddy were hitting the town before they fucked off outta here. Going to Reno I heard."

"He's still in town, right?"

"Yeah." He paused. "I'm pretty sure he is."

"Oh, Jesus, you fucking pothead. Where is he?" Collins started pacing the laneway, gripping the phone harder.

"Yeah, relax, man. This guy I know said he was with his buddy Watkins. Remember Watkins? Fat, greasy fucker. I always thought he was a baby-banger, too."

"Get to the point, Geez, before I track you down and kick the shit out of you."

"Whoa. Not cool. He was at this burger place I'm at right now. 'Bout an hour ago."

Collins shook her head and kicked at the wall. "I don't give a sweet shit where he was an hour ago. I want to know where he is right now."

"What am I supposed to be, psychic or something?"

"Okay, screw it, Geez. Don't text me again, okay? You've become less than useless." Collins started walking out of the lane.

"Hey, Detective. My hundred bucks?"

"You didn't give me anything. I don't give you anything. Now piss off."

"I told you I could get him."

Collins stopped walking. "No, you said you thought you had something. 'Thought' isn't a word you should throw around loosely." She looked around. "So do you or do you not have something? Do you know where he is?"

"I know where he'll be. That good enough?"

"That's more like it. Where, and when?" She took a pen and paper from her pocket.

"I said they were in the burger joint, right? I

overheard them talking."

She heard Geezer yawn. "Am I keeping you awake?"

"It was good weed. I got to grab another burger."

"Keep talking."

"Yeah, yeah. I'll have a double cheeseburger, fries and one of them frozen orange things."

"You talking to me?"

"What? No. Getting food. Where was I?"

"You were telling me where the pedo twins were going to be, and when."

"Oh, yeah. The guy, Wheeler's friend, said something about hitting' a pool hall after picking' up some weed."

Collins finger-combed her hair in frustration. "You're really short on specifics, Geez."

"Hang on a sec. The weed place I don't know. I mean, I know a bunch of places I could go and hypothetically get weed, but I don't know where they're going tonight."

"The pool hall then."

"The place out west, across from the donut place. You know it?"

Collins scribbled on her pad. "I can find it."

"I'll send you the address. When do I get my money?"

A text message with the address popped up on her screen, and she hung up. She looked at her watch. "Tonight it is."

The Woman in the El Camino sat in a parking lot about four hundred feet away from Collins. She lowered the parabolic mike and made a note. "Geezer. It's been a long time. Wish I could have heard your side of the conversation."

Collins walked into the squadron and found Hastings, Wilson and Barnes standing around her desk. "What's going on, guys?"

"That's my question," said Barnes. "Wilson has told

me an interesting story about a visitor in the night." He looked at Hastings. "And apparently this visitor cleared one of your cold cases. You've managed to duck almost all of them."

Collins moved to hang her jacket over the back of her chair. "Weird, right?"

"Stop." Hastings took her gently by the arm. "Don't sit there."

"What?"

"A tech is on his way up. According to Wilson, this person was hanging here for about an hour. Had to leave a print or two."

Collins backed away from her desk. "Okay. That makes sense." She looked around. "Where do I sit?"

Hastings smiled. "My lap has room."

"Boss, that sounds very much like sexual harassment." Collins looked at Hastings, then smiled. "Keep cracking on to me, and I'll take you to Florida with me."

"I thought you were going to Arizona."

A young tech arrived and they gave him space. He looked around. "What are we looking for?"

"Dust my desk for prints," said Collins. "Check them against mine for reference. You'll find them on file. How long will this take?"

The tech looked at the paper on the desk. "About an hour. Go get some lunch. I'll be finished when you get back."

Collins swung her jacket back on. "Sounds like a plan. Hastings, you want to join me?"

"Oh, Jesus. More grease, right?" He pulled on his jacket. "Barnes, there's a defib on this floor? Make sure it's charged up for me when I get back."

Hastings followed Collins out of the station. "Where we off to, granny?"

"There's a new burger place that puts bacon and fried egg on them." She kissed her fingertips. "Fantastic. A work of art. I'm buying."

"My cholesterol is going to hit 300 I keep doing this."

"We all die."

"I'd like to put that off for as long as possible."

Collins laughed. "Pussy."

The tech had finished by the time they returned. He had his samples collected and his kit packed as she approached her desk.

"How long for results?"

"It's pretty automated. Give me ten minutes."

"That it?"

"I'm very good." He smiled and disappeared to his lab.

Collins dropped her jacket over her chair and sat. She opened the Dunne file with her notes and opened a word processing program. "Easiest cold case I've ever had."

"Easier than the four you tossed my way? 'Cause those were extremely easy, for you."

"Almost." She started typing her report. "This is going to be a weird write-up though. I'm going to give credit to a phantom lady."

"You're not."

Collins smiled. "I'll hand this in the day before I leave. Barnes will have a cow, and there'll be nothing he can do about it."

Hastings shook his head. "We never really know the people we work with. I'm going to lean on the tech. I want to know who the serial killer is."

"You think she's the one?"

"So do you. Makes the Taser story a little more reasonable."

"Except they didn't exist," said Collins. "Or so I've been told."

"So she invented something. I saw the video. She isn't a large woman. She would need to incapacitate someone from a distance if they were any larger than her."

"So tell Wilson to start looking at psychopaths who held electrical engineering degrees in the seventies."

Hastings chewed the inside of his cheek. "It *does*

sound stupid when you put it that way."

The tech came in the squad room with a manila envelope in his hands. "Detective Collins." He handed her the envelope. "I told you I was fast."

"Thorough?" She opened the envelope and slid out the results. She quickly read the single sheet. "Just me and Hastings?" She handed the paper back. "You missed something."

"I missed nothing. Whoever was sitting at your desk last night was very careful."

"They would be, wouldn't they," said Hastings. "So, back to square one."

Collins looked at the paper and dropped it on her desk. "Okay. Thanks. If you discover that you've made a mistake, tell me. I'll be disappointed, not angry."

The tech smiled. "I don't make mistakes. Have a great day, Detective."

Collins scratched the back of her head, puzzled. "Hey, Wilson," she yelled.

The FBI agent lifted his head and scowled. He dropped what he was doing and walked over to Collins' desk. "What?"

"That woman. Was she wearing gloves?" She pointed at her desk. "No prints. Anywhere." She handed the report to Wilson, who scanned it quickly and handed it back.

"Not a clue. Wasn't paying attention. Looks like she was pretty careful." He smiled. "I've got to get back to it. Good luck."

She tossed the report on her desk. "Shit."

"Don't worry about it, Collins. Finish that report and piss off home. I'll cover for you if Barnes is looking."

She rubbed her forehead. "Not a bad idea."

"Want to grab a movie tonight? I'm sure there's something playing with explosions and guns."

"No. I'm going to take it easy. Thanks." She closed the file. "And I'll do the report tomorrow."

"Semi-retirement."

"I still work harder in four hours than you do in

eight, kid. And don't forget it." She pulled on her jacket. "See you tomorrow."

Chapter 18

The Woman was half asleep in her car when Collins left the station.

"Oh, shit" she righted the seat and started the engine. Collins got into her car on the far side of the lot and started it, exhaust obscuring it for a moment. The Woman put her El Camino into gear and started moving, thinking that Collins had left. A breath of wind blew the exhaust to one side and the Woman applied the brakes.

Collins sat in her car for a few more minutes, the Woman about a hundred feet behind her.

"What in the hell are you waiting for, Collins?" The Woman looked around. The parking lot, large enough for at least 300 cars, was less than half full.

She felt exposed. She looked at the analog clock on the dashboard and made a decision. At not quite 2 pm Collins would probably be going home. Maybe an opportunity to find out where Wheeler would be.

She popped the car into gear and left the lot, Collins still warming up her car.

Collins rubbed her hands together, trying to get warmth to her fingertips. "I fucking hate winter." She watched a black El Camino pull out of the lot and slapped the dash. "Warm up, you piece of shit." Frost built up on the inside of the windshield. She flipped the heat switch to *defrost* and cranked the fan to full speed. Half-moons of clear glass slowly spread out.

When there was enough visibility to drive, she pulled out of the parking lot and pointed home.

Barnes walked down the stairs from his office and headed to Collins' desk. "Where is she?"

Hastings smiled. "Started her retirement early." He

laughed at the look on Barnes' face. "She took off. Was feeling a bit under the weather. What's up?"

"An investigation has been launched into the unauthorized entry to this squad room. We need her statement."

"Her statement? Like she's a suspect?"

"She's a witness. I saw the video from the lane out back." Barnes looked at Hastings. "I'm going to need your statement also."

Hastings wiped the corners of his mouth. "Sure. I wasn't here that night and saw fuck all out back. You want more of a statement than that?"

"Don't be a smart-ass, Hastings. This is pretty serious shit. Can you imagine if any suspect could wander in, steal or alter evidence and walk out again? Jesus."

"Why didn't Wilson stop her? He was here that night."

"Damned good question. Wilson, get over here," yelled Barnes. "Hastings, find out who was here last night from our team."

"What the hell are you yelling about, Barnes?"

"That woman who waltzed through here last night - why didn't you challenge her?"

"Why should I," asked Wilson. "She swiped in. Thought she was one of yours. Fuck, is your security that lax?"

Barnes grabbed a phone off the desk. "Get an IT geek. I want to know every access card swiped in last night from 5 to midnight." He slammed the handset down. "Hastings, who was here?"

Hastings had two cops with him. "Detectives Owen and Hargreaves. Gents, tell Cap what you told me."

"She was talking with Wilson here. Figured she was a Fed. They seemed pretty familiar with each other," said Owen.

Hargreaves nodded. "We talked last night. Didn't think that much of it."

Barnes had his hands on his hips. "So what did she look like?"

Hargreaves shrugged. "Like I said, we didn't pay much attention."

Barnes waved them away. "Right. So she walks in, fucks with stuff, walks out and doesn't leave any prints. Unacceptable."

A young techie-type walked in and cleared his throat. "Captain Barnes?"

"What?"

The young guy held out a sheet of paper. "Log of all the swipes from last night, sir."

Barnes grabbed the paper. He scanned down the list, then looked back at the tech. "All of them?"

"Ev-every one, sir."

Barnes nodded. "Thanks. Take off."

Hastings looked over his shoulder. "What's it show?"

"Has Collins ever report her badge stolen?"

"She was complaining about losing it yesterday. Showed up on her desk today."

Barnes handed the paper to Hastings. "Collins' card

was used last night."

"She wasn't here, though. I talked to her at home last night. Checking up on her."

"Call her. Get her back here. We need to talk to her."

Hastings looked at Barnes for a couple of seconds, then nodded. "I'll track her down."

The Woman sat in her car a half a block down the street from Collins' apartment building. She was just settling in for a wait when Collins rolled up and ran from her car to the apartment building. The Woman looked at the time. She pulled a piece of paper out of her pocket and read the address. "Let's hope you're home, Wheeler, getting ready for a night out."

Collins plugged in the kettle and sat at her kitchen table, face in her hands, thinking about what she was going to do. Her phone started ringing. She looked at the display. Hastings. Collins turned off the ringer and got up and made a cup of coffee.

The El Camino rolled up in front of Wheeler's house half an hour later. The Woman got out and slowly walked up the front steps and onto the porch. She stepped over the screen door, now completely off its hinges. She pushed the front door open, the hinges complaining against the rust. She stopped and listened. There was no noise coming from the house. She took out a gun, entered and swept through the living room, down the hallway and into the kitchen. Remains of a sandwich and an empty beer bottle sat on the kitchen counter.

The house was empty.

"Fuck." She holstered her gun, took out her phone and scrolled through the numbers in her contact list. She stared at it for a minute, then called. When the person on the other end answered she could hear the deafening noise of ten-pin bowling and arcade music.

"Who's this?"

"Geezer, I'm looking for Wheeler."

"You gotta talk louder. I can't hear you. Who is this?"

"Where's Wheeler?"

"Fuck it's noisy here. I can barely hear you. This Collins? I already told ya. The pool hall 'cross from the donut shop on the west end. Not now, but later tonight. Why you asking' me again? I still want my money. You owe me."

The Woman pressed her phone to her head. "Pool hall, west end of town. Got it. Thanks." She hung up and dropped the phone in her pocket. "I think I know the place."

Hastings hung up, shook his head and looked up the stairs toward Barnes office. "Jesus, Collins, what are you doing?" He walked up to the captain's office and knocked on the doorframe. "I'm going to go look for her. She's not answering."

"Bring her back here when you find her."

"You think she's got something to do with this?"

Barnes shook his head and pointed at a chair. "Sit for a second."

Hastings lowered himself into the chair. "What?"

"You've gotten pretty close to Collins the last year. And that's good. She's always been a loner. Very effective on her own, so I haven't made much of a deal about it." He scrubbed his face. "This job has been her life, especially since her husband was killed. I'm worried about her. She's not going to have much of anything after she retires."

"She'll be okay. I'll keep in touch. We'll play bridge. Strip poker." Hastings laughed and stood. "Let me go get her and see what she knows about all this, if anything."

"Yeah, go."

Hastings parked his car outside Collins apartment building. It was getting dark. The streetlights had just turned on. He looked up at her window. The lights were off.

He got out of the car and buzzed her apartment at the front door. He waited a couple of minutes, then buzzed all of them. A couple of people yelled something through the squawk box, but at least one buzzed to let him in.

Collins lived on the first floor. Hastings knocked on her door a couple of times. Then crossed the hall to the building Super's door, held his badge up to the peephole and knocked.

A Pat Morita look-alike opened the door. "What can I do for you, Detective?"

Hastings jabbed his thumb over his shoulder. "Worried about Collins. She's not answering the phone. Seemed off today."

The super nodded and produced a ring of keys. "I noticed the same thing." He opened the door and stood to one side while Hastings entered. "You're on your own. I don't go in. The door locks behind you."

Hastings nodded and closed the door behind him.

"Collins, you in here?" He walked around the still apartment. It was empty. It didn't take long to check that out. The place was small. "Where are you, granny?"

He poked around the small living room. He saw a scrap of folded paper on the table beside the lounge chair. He unfolded it and read what she had scribbled. "Wheeler? Oh, Jesus."

Chapter 19

Collins drove her car into a small parking lot behind the pool hall. She turned off the ignition and sat in the stillness for a moment. She closed her eyes and took a deep breath, slowly exhaling it through her nose. "It's killing time."

She opened her door and her phone rang. She looked at the display and grunted. "Not a good time, Geez."

"Did you just call me?"

"Yeah, about three hours ago."

"More like five hours ago, but that's not what I was talking about. Less than an hour ago, from a different phone, looking for Wheeler."

"Bad weed, Geez. I've got to go. You want your

money, stop acting like an idiot. Don't call me again."

She hung up and got out of her car. She was parked behind a green Corolla. She peered in the back window and saw a couple bags of clothes in the back seat. She smiled. "Got ya."

Two dumpsters were pushed up against the back wall of the pool hall, a space about two feet wide between them. Collins looked up at the light pole on the far corner of the lot, spilling its dim rays across the cars and leaving a deep shadow between the dumpsters.

She stepped in between them and squatted down in the dark.

"Oh, Jesus, that stinks." She stood with her hand over her mouth and nose and stepped out from between them and around to the front of the pool hall.

There were six pool tables at the back. When she walked in two were occupied, one of them with Wheeler and who she assumed was Watkins. She slid onto a stool on the bar and tapped on the counter. "Lite beer." She watched her target rack the balls. "And a bag of chips."

Wheeler set the balls and stood back, bumping into Watkins. He looked down at his friend. "Back up, asshole. My break."

He bent over and lined up with the cue ball, struck it, and watched none of the balls drop. "Son of a bitch." He grabbed his bottle of beer off the side of the table, limped out of the way and leaned against the wall beside a rack of cues. "My lucky day."

Watkins lined up and dropped a stripe. "You're foot okay? Limping more than you were this morning."

"Oxy's wearing off. Need to get some more."

Watkins angled off the bank and dropped another stripe. "So you never told me. How in the ever lovin' fuck did you get out? You're a lucky man, Wheeler."

"Damned if I know. Not complaining, though."

"I figured you for at least fifteen to twenty."

Wheeler shrugged and watched Watkins drop

another ball. "Yeah, me too. Prosecutor screwed up, somehow. I don't even know how. Public defender came to me and said it was over. I was free to walk." Wheeler grinned. "My momma didn't raise no dummies. I fucking walked."

"He must been pissed he missed out on the trial dollars."

Wheeler tipped back his beer. "Yeah, he was pissed, all right."

Collins moved closer to the tables with her beer and her chips, keeping a support pillar between her and the table. She was close enough to hear them talk.

Watkins sunk another ball and cackled. "You're going to owe me big for this one. Hey, maybe the cop fucked up."

Wheeler twisted the top off another beer and chuckled. "That bitch scares the hell out of me. Tenacious as a terrier."

"Fuck her."

"Not even with your dick, Watkins."

The El Camino drove past the pool hall parking lot. The Woman saw the green Corolla. She stopped, backed up and parked. She got out, her breath fogging the air. She took the suppressor out of her pocket and threaded it onto the end of her handgun. She looked around and stepped into the shadows between the dumpsters.

Watkins dropped the last striped ball, then the eight ball and Wheeler handed him a twenty.

Wheeler set the balls up again. "Double or nothing."

"Double it is. So what's your plans?" Watkins looked at the cue ball and stepped out of the way. "You break."

"Plans about what?"

"Where you going? You sure as hell can't hang around here."

Wheeler broke and dropped a solid ball.

"Everything I own is in my car. I'm heading south tonight."

Collins nursed her beer while she eavesdropped on Wheeler and Watkins. Hastings tried to call her twice, and both times, she declined the call.

Hastings sat in his car in front of Collins' apartment, waiting. He called her cell phone again, and again she dumped it to voicemail. "Jesus, Collins. Quit ducking me. We need to talk."

He dropped his phone on the passenger's seat, then grabbed it and dialed the number for the lab. "This is Detective Hastings. I need you to do a locate on a cell phone. I know I'm supposed to have a warrant, but this is Detective Collins' phone. I'm worried about her. She's missing. She might be in danger of self-harm." He recited Collins' number. Call me when you get a location. *Immediately* when you get a location."

Watkins watched as Wheeler sank three more solid

balls in a row, then just miss a fourth. "Where south? New Orleans would be fun."

Wheeler took his beer and limped to the wall. "I'm going on my own. Wherever I go, you don't." He tipped back the bottle for a mouthful. "And sure as fuck not New Orleans. Place creeps me out with all those graves above ground. Phoenix, maybe."

"Too hot for me." Watkins lined up on a striped ball and dropped it in the corner pocket, the cue ball slowly rolling back into a perfect position for a follow-up. "And way too dry. You don't even sweat there. You could be completely dehydrated, and you'd never know."

Wheeler nodded. "That's why I like it. Humidity brings crotch rot."

Watkins missed his shot and stepped aside for Wheeler. "And who wants crotch rot, right?"

Wheeler knocked the cue ball into the corner pocket and threw his cue stick onto the table. "Mother-fuck." He took out his wallet and gave Watkins another $20.

"I hate this game."

"We outta here?"

Wheeler finished his beer "Yeah. The tables are bent. You need a lift somewhere?"

"Where ya going?"

"Find a little something to tide me over on the trip." He grabbed his crotch. "I got the need."

"You're a freak, man. I'm good."

"So what ya gonna do, Watkins?"

"Head down the block a bit, score some bud, hit a strip joint. *I* like 'em with little titties." He finished his beer and left it on the edge of the pool table. "Let's blow this fuckin' place."

Wheeler nodded. "But I gotta piss first."

Hastings sat in his car, drumming his fingers on the steering wheel. "How long does it take to track a goddamned phone?" He opened his phone to call the tech back when it rang.

"Detective Hastings?"

"Yeah, spit it out."

"I've got an address for you."

Hastings wrote it on a pad of paper and hung up. "Don't do anything stupid, Collins." He put his car in gear and headed to the west end of town.

Chapter 20

Collins waited until Wheeler entered the men's room, then slipped out of the pool hall. She walked around to the back parking lot, looked briefly at the black space between the dumpsters, and shook her head. She walked past Wheeler's puke-green Corolla and settled behind her car. She slid the Beretta out of her ankle holster and attached the suppressor.

The pool hall noise spilled out of the open door. Collins looked around the fender of her car and watched Wheeler and Watkins walk out.

"This is it, Watkins. If you're ever in Phoenix, don't look me up. Or Tucson. Or maybe I'll go to New Mexico."

"Any place warm is good, I guess." Watkins gave

Wheeler a bro handshake/hug. "Catch you later, dude. Or not. Keep your dick out of trouble." He patted Wheeler on the shoulder and headed down the road.

Collins quietly ejected the magazine, confirmed the load and re-inserted it. Wheeler limped over to his car and bent down to unlock the door when Collins stood up.

He took a step back. "You? What the fuck?"

"Enough is enough. I should have done you in the farmhouse. Would have been a lot easier."

Wheeler stutter-stepped, then turned to run. In a smooth, rapid motion, the Woman stepped out from between the dumpsters, arm extended and shot him in the back with a Taser. Wheeler fell forward, spasms wracking his muscles. The Woman walked over to Wheeler, retrieved the wires and barbs with her gloved hand and shot him in the back, twice.

Collins trained her Beretta on the Woman. The streetlight shone from the Woman's left. Her hood cast a shadow, obscuring Collins' view of her face.

"Freeze, and keep your hands where I can see them."

"You don't want to do this."

"Like hell I don't."

"I did you a favor."

Hastings was less than a mile away when his radio came alive. *"All units, reported shooting at Rupert's Pool Hall on the corner of Clayton and Central. Two shots heard."*

Hastings flicked the switch and lit up his blue and reds. He floored it and flipped open his phone, redialing the last number he'd been trying to reach for hours. It rang out to voicemail again. "Jesus Christ, Collins." He threw his phone on the passenger's seat and skidded his car into a corner. "What in the hell are you up to?"

Collins took her eyes off the Woman for a split second when her phone rang. That's all it took. The Woman pulled the trigger on the Taser, and the second of three cartridges fired, hitting Collins in the chest with both barbs.

"Arghhh" She looked down at the wires strung from her chest as she lost all control of her muscles. Her back arched as she fell, firing a round into the pavement by her feet. Her jaws clenched, and she bit her tongue. She banged her head on the pavement, and her back arched further. Spittle foamed at the corners of her mouth and her eyes rolled back in her head.

The Woman walked over with her Taser in one hand and her handgun in the other. She poked Collins in the ribs with the toe of her boot. "Sorry, but you didn't leave me much choice." She dropped the cartridge on Collins' chest, then thought better of it and collected the wires and barbs. "That's going to sting for a few days. Make sure you take good care of it. We wouldn't want any unsightly scars now, would we?"

Collins gasped for breath.

"Just relax into it, Collins. It'll ease off in a couple of minutes." Sirens sounded in the distance. "That's my cue. I need to leave."

Collins fought against her weak muscles and tried to lift her gun.

The Woman nodded. "Thanks for reminding me." She picked the gun from Collins' hand. "You wouldn't want to have that on you when the cops show up. You'll thank me later."

Collins fought to sit. "Fuuuuuuuck." She rolled over onto her front and tried to force herself to her knees. She looked over, through unfocussed eyes, at Wheeler, face down on the pavement, a pool of blood spreading out under his rapidly cooling body.

She made it to her knees, and the Woman left Wheeler's body and put a foot in the middle of her back and pressed her back onto the pavement. "Get up before I leave, and I'll zap you again. I really don't want to, but I've got one shot left in this thing and I will." She turned to leave, then stopped and looked down at Collins. "You might think about hitting the gym. You're losing muscle tone."

The hooded Woman returned to Wheeler's body and rolled him over onto his back. She grabbed him under the armpits and dragged him to her El Camino. The last thing Collins saw before she blacked out was the Woman hoisting his body into the back of her car.

Chapter 21

Hastings slowed as he reached the pool hall. He turned into the parking lot, his headlights playing over Collins. "Son of a bitch."

He jumped out of the car and ran to Collins body. She groaned and rolled onto her side as he approached. He took her by the arm and helped her up. "What in the hell happened?"

Collins leaned over, her hands on her knees. She slowly straightened and leaned on Wheeler's car. "How did you know I was here?"

Hastings put an arm around her and led her to his car. He opened the passenger's door and sat her down, her feet on the pavement. He squatted down in front of her and took her hands in his. "Seriously, Deb, what in the hell has happened here? Are you hurt?"

Collins eased her hands free and dry scrubbed her face. She winced as she briefly touched her shirt where the woman tagged her with the Taser. "Pride, more than anything else." She sighed and closed her eyes. "You're going to have to call this in?"

"What's 'this'? What were you doing this far away from home?"

Collins pulled herself to her feet and led Hastings to a pool of blood by the dumpsters. "Tape this off. Someone was shot here."

"I heard. What did you see? Where's your service revolver?"

Collins held out her hands. "Hey, I clocked off hours ago. My .38 is at home in the gun safe. I was …" She trailed off and cleared her throat. "This is a mess."

"Who was shot?"

Collins patted her pockets and took out her cigarettes. She lit one, dragged deep and exhaled with a sigh. "Call it in and give me a couple of minutes, Hastings. I need to collect myself." She held up her cigarette. "Let me finish this, and we'll talk." She walked over to her car. Hastings watched her for a second, then got on his radio.

She looked over her shoulder at him, spooling out crime scene tape, and dialled a number on her phone. "Geezer, where are you?"

"Yo, you're interrupting me. Where's my money?"

"I've got more for you. I need you to keep an eye open for a black El Camino. Vintage. Late sixties, I think."

"More money?"

"Another hundred." Collins looked back at Hastings. He was still busy.

"Sure. No problem." Geezer paused. "The fuck's an El Camino?"

"Jesus, fucking kids nowadays. Like a car and a pickup truck had a baby. Can't miss it."

"License plate?"

"No idea. A woman's driving it. Last seen by that pool hall you told me about. Call or text me as soon as you know where it is. Any time, day or night."

She hung up, took one long and final drag on her cigarette and ground it out under her heel. She slid her hands into her jacket pockets and slowly walked back to Hastings.

He glanced at her, tied off the last piece of police tape and tossed the roll in the trunk of his car. "You okay?"

A couple of uniforms managed the crowd outside, diverting traffic away from the lot. They split the crowd and allowed a crime scene tech wagon into the parking lot. Collins shrugged. "I'm as good as can be expected. I'll run the plates in the parking lot, see what comes up."

"No, you're sitting in the car. Stay out of the way. I'll run this." He looked at her for a second and shook his head. "I'm going to have some questions when we're finished here."

Collins looked at the green Corolla and nodded. "Whatever."

"Go. Sit. I'll do the cars now."

She leaned against Hastings car with her arms crossed, watching him work. He opened an app on his phone and entered a license plate number, make and model of car. As the owner information came up on the screen he wrote it in his pad for future reference.

He moved to the front of the Corolla and entered the plate number. The results appeared on his phone and he took a half step back. He looked at Collins and back at his phone.

"Collins, come here."

"Ah, shit." She pushed herself off Hastings car and walked over, head down in thought. "Let me guess. Wheeler's car?"

Hastings licked his lips and rubbed his forehead. "That his blood?"

"It wasn't me. Someone else shot him and - and when I tried to intercede, she..." Collins paused and rested her hand on her chest. "She stopped me. Knocked me out."

"She? Seriously? The woman from behind the station, right? Fucking hell, Collins. What in the hell have you gotten yourself into? What aren't you telling me? What were you doing here?"

She held her hands up in surrender. "Whoa, Hastings. So intense." She lowered them and looked over her shoulder at the uniforms behind her. "Not so loud, okay? Yeah, I was following Wheeler. I wanted to drop-kick him in the nuts and maybe give him an extra-generous circumcision. But I sure as hell didn't shoot him." She held open her jacket. "No weapon. Check me for GSR if you want." She stood, waiting, in the cold, for a response. "Come on, Hastings. Hurry up. I don't have the body fat insulation you've got."

"Just go sit in the car. We'll talk later."

"Let's talk now, I might be dead later. I'm old, ya know."

"Tomorrow. It's getting late. You should go home

and have a drink. A real one. No lite beer. Then get some rest."

Collins nodded. "You figure out what happened here, you let me know, okay?" She backed away and got in her car. She flipped open her phone and pressed redial. "Geez, you hear anything yet?"

"Who's this?"

"Fuck off, Geezer. Where's the El Camino?"

"Collins. Didn't recognize your voice. Why are you whispering?"

"The car. Where's the fucking car?"

"Come on, Detective. It's been less than an hour. I haven't heard anything yet."

"Listen, you shit. Get off your pot-infused ass and hit the streets yourself. I need to know where that car is." She closed her phone and pulled out of the parking lot.

The Woman drove east, debating her next move. There was too much attention with this one. The lake would be the best decision, but this wasn't the time to change her methods.

She kept it near high-traffic areas. The danger level was higher, but the message had to be sent. These assholes would still be alive if the justice system wasn't so fucked up.

Even near midnight the traffic on I-75 wasn't light. She exited north at John Lodge freeway and took the first side street. She pulled up beside an empty lot and put the car in neutral and engaged the handbrake. She left it running. Stopping and starting the car would draw more attention than it just sitting there, idling.

She grunted Wheelers stiffening corpse from the back of the El Camino and dumped it among the rubbish in the empty lot.

Collins parked and turned off the ignition and sat in front of her apartment. "Fucking hell." She exhaled slowly and rubbed her face. "Well, at least I don't have to worry about the fucking pedo anymore."

She hunched into her jacket as she ran into her apartment building, She kicked the radiator and threw her jacket on a chair, rubbing her hands to warm them up.

She took off her blouse and bra and looked at the angry, red burns on her chest. They were smaller than the ones she'd seen on the medical examiner's photos. She looked at her jacket and back at her chest. She picked it up and was examining the small holes in it when her phone rang.

"Who's this?"

"You okay? Taking care of those burn marks?"

"Listen, bitch, who in the hell are you?"

"One day, one day. For now, just a reminder to stay as far away from that serial case as you can. Keep clear of it, okay?"

"What?"

"Just keep clear, old girl." The Woman laughed. "Old girl. That's funny. Look, it's late, and I need sleep. A couple of busy days coming up. You should get some rest, too. I'll talk to you later."

Collins looked at her phone. The call came from a blocked number. She tapped the edge of the phone on the table and thought about her next move. Thought about the balance between finding out who this fucking Woman was, and revealing to the force how much she already knew.

She looked at the time and scribbled it on a piece of paper.

Chapter 22

Collins walked into the squad room the next morning to find Hastings pawing through the papers on her desk. "What?"

Hastings looked up and smiled. He moved to the other side of her desk. "Looking for the Wheeler case file. He goes on the board now."

Collins hung her jacket on the back of her chair and sat at her desk. "You need a body before it goes up on the board. Maybe the crazy bitch just wounded him and is at this very moment holding him in a basement somewhere, pulling out his fingernails and shoving toothpicks up his urethra." She pulled the file from under a stack of notes and handed it to him.

Hastings winced. "Kipling was right. Don't let them

give you to the women." He saluted her with the file. "A black and white found his body in an empty lot this morning. Strictly speaking, I'm sure some of the neighbors knew he was there, but they don't like chatting to us that much."

"Same place as the others?"

Hastings waggled his hand. "About a mile from where Packer's body was dumped. And he's dead. All fingernails intact. I'll have the ME look for toothpicks in the dick, if you think that's really a possibility."

"I don't think that's necessary. Why aren't you at the drop site?"

"The FBI are working the scene. I *wanted* to go, but I was asked to have a word with you."

"I need a coffee for this." She grabbed her cup and looked at the mess in it.

"Let's go for a walk and I'll buy you a good one." He looked around the room. "Better we talk about some of this outside anyway, right?" He nodded for her to follow. "Grab your jacket."

"Hang on, I've got to do something first." She took a scrap of paper from her pocket and emailed the IT techs, asking for any information on the call she'd received from the woman.

"Good to go." She grabbed her jacket and followed Hastings outside. "The usual place." She lit a cigarette while she walked. "And take your time. I can't smoke this there."

Hastings looked up at the blue sky. "Nice weather for a change."

"We're talking about the weather now?" She tapped her cigarette and dropped some ash. "I thought we had more important things to discuss."

Hastings grunted. "Fine. So tell me about what happened last night."

"I bumped into him in the parking lot and somebody else killed him before I had a chance to."

"Not even as a joke, Collins. He's on the board now and I'm going to need a description."

"I've never seen her face. She does this thing with

her hood that obscures it. She's been doing that a long time."

"How do you know?"

"She's had a lot of practice." She exhaled smoke through her nose. "I can give you rough build and size, hair color, but she's either stayed in the shadows or had that damned hoodie on all the time." She dropped the cigarette on the sidewalk and ground it out with her heel.

Hastings ordered coffee, then held a chair for Collins and sat across from her on the patio. "So what happened last night?"

Collins exhaled. "Pretty much what you already know, pup. I tracked him down with the help of some of my CIs. I was planning to bust kneecaps, maybe crush his nuts, one at a time. Then that crazy lady stepped out of the shadows and iced him."

The server brought their coffee. Hastings waited until he had left before continuing. He leaned forward. "*Iced*, Collins? Give me something here."

She blew on her coffee and took a sip. "I didn't kill him. I'm not sad he's dead, but I didn't kill him. She came out from between the two dumpsters back there and put two in his back. Then she overpowered me, and as I was fading, I saw her dragging him away."

"Man, don't tell the story like that to Barnes."

Collins laughed. "I'll temper it a bit." She held his eyes while she took another drink. "So, what's this mean for me? Am I on suspension?"

Hastings almost spit his coffee. He swallowed, then laughed. "Oh, quite the opposite. You're the only person who has had any contact with this nut job. Wilson has lobbied for you to be on the task force. Barnes wants to talk to you first, but you're going to be going out with a bang."

"And here I thought he was going to fire me." She finished her coffee and stood. "I should probably get back and talk to the Cap."

"Keep the kneecap-busting and nut-crushing out of the story, okay?"

Collins took the stairs two at a time and knocked on Captain Barnes' doorframe. "Hey, Cap. You wanted to yell at me?"

He pointed at a chair with his pen. "Pull up a stool. Has Hastings talked to you?"

"Yeah, and I don't want to re-hash all of it again."

Barnes nodded. "I'm just curious about one thing. The case details I can get from the reports. I want to know why this killer is stalking you. Messing through your desk, interrupting your smoke time and now picking off the one person on the face of this green earth who you wanted dead."

"I'm kinda curious about that myself." She leaned back in the chair and scratched the back of her head. "I've been wracking my brain, trying to think of any connections I might have with her."

"Nothing?"

Collins waggled her hand. "A couple of the older cases I worked on, but not as primary. Nothing else.

She's taken a liking to me, for some reason."

Barnes nodded, satisfied. "Good. Get Wilson to exploit that."

"So you're not pissed I tracked Wheeler down last night?"

Barnes echoed the hand waggle. "Not sure I wouldn't have done the same thing. Hastings tells me you didn't have a weapon with you."

"Just wanted to have a word with the guy." She scratched at her chin. "Maybe let him know what it's like to tangle with someone his own size instead of little kiddies."

"His own size? He is—was—a good foot taller than you and at least fifty pounds heavier."

"Excuse me. At least a hundred pounds heavier." She chuckled. "I'm upset, really, that I didn't get that chance to take him apart."

"Wilson is going to want to get all those details."

"So that's the official disciplinary action? Making me work with the fucking feds?"

Barnes laughed. "I thought you wanted to be on it. End your career on a high."

"I thought I did that with Wheeler behind bars. This is a good second, I guess."

"The very Special Agent Wilson has been briefed and is expecting you. They're all out at the dump site. Catch up with him when he gets back."

"I'll be out back screwing up my lungs if anyone is looking for me."

Barnes watched her leave, then picked up his phone. "Hastings, I need to talk to you. My office."

He flipped through papers on his desk, looking up when Hastings walked in. "I talked to Collins. She told me nothing. What do you know?"

"I rolled up on the-"

"Yeah, let's start there. You live hell and gone away from the pool hall, and it was way after your shift ended. How and why were you there?"

Hastings fiddled with his watch. "She's been a worry to me lately, sitting on her ass working those cold cases you gave her. That's really not her. You know it."

"Guns blazing, shooting first, taking names later, I know. If her clearance rate wasn't so high I would have put an end to it years ago. So you were babysitting her?"

"Loosely, I guess. I had the techs track her phone last night. Probably against procedures, but she left early, and I couldn't reach her. She wasn't at her apartment." He picked at his teeth. "Overboard?"

"Maybe not. Retirement is always a rough time for career cops. She hardened after her husband died. Didn't let many people in. You were one of the closest to her."

"What do you mean 'were'? I still am. Except she's never told me what happened to her husband."

Barnes grimaced. "She'll kill me."

"Then I'll ask her."

"Nah, she won't tell you." Barnes rubbed his mouth. "Okay, you should know. He was on the Fire

Department. An arsonist who had skipped bail lit up a warehouse. He was trapped. Her husband went in to get him and was killed in the process. Icing on the cake is the arsonist evaded all of the cops on the scene and lit an elementary school the next week. Killed a bunch of kids and seriously injured more. A couple of teachers died. The Principal barely made it out alive."

"That's just a weird coincidence."

"Isn't it? And now the killer of felons who happens to be on the street on technicalities is courting her." Barnes leaned forward. "And I've had a thought. These killings go back to the seventies, right?"

"That's what it looks like. Why?"

"Forty years on a slow burn is a long time. You know that. The killer must be getting up there. It's an organized, methodical process the killer is following. That leans toward starting in their mid-to late twenties, which would put them into their seventies. Maybe she's looking at Collins as a recruit, someone to take over."

Hastings was shaking his head before Barnes finished talking. "No. It's something else. That's not Collins."

"You telling me that you would have been surprised if it was Collins killing that scum behind the pool hall? We'll all kill if the motivation is strong enough. You know that."

Chapter 23

Wilson intercepted Collins as she came down the stairs from Barnes' office. "So Barnes explained things to you?"

"Yeah. Why?"

"Thanks for joining the team."

"Barnes intimated I didn't have much of a choice." She took her seat. "Not that I mind. Where are we?"

Wilson dropped files on her desk. "These are the original reports for the victims. I need you to review them."

Collins flipped open the first one. "Yeah, I was the detective working these when they were cold cases. I know them."

"That's why you're here."

She dropped the file on her desk. "So I'm essentially back on the cold cases. Lovely."

"Not really, Collins. You were looking at them as stand-alone, individual cases. Look at them with fresh eyes. They're linked cases. Pick one aspect, focus on that." Wilson tapped her desk with his fingertips. "Really glad to have you on board." He smiled and went back to his desk.

Collins looked at the pile of files she thought she had put behind her and shoved them across her desk. "Fuck this. I need that smoke."

Chapter 24

Collins leaned against the back wall, eyes half closed enjoying her cigarette. Her phone vibrated in her pocket and she absent-mindedly looked at it.

Think I found your car.

She stubbed out her cigarette and called. "What you got for me, Geez?"

"Who's this?"

"Jesus, Geez, who's your dealer? You must be getting really good weed."

"Collins, right? I found your car. It's a really sweet 1967 El Camino. Black. Like you said. That's probably it, right?"

"Where?" Collins left the lane behind the station and headed to her car. "Exactly."

"It went into a garage of this old house. Bad side of town. Even for me."

"Yeah, whatever. Just send the address and get out of there."

She hung up, and her phone buzzed with a message. She looked at the address and frowned. She typed it into the map app on her phone and chuckled. "Jesus. Two blocks from the Ninth. What balls. I love it."

Wilson tapped on Hastings' desk. "Detective, where's Collins?"

Hastings looked from his work. "Thought she was with you. You lose her already? You'll learn. She's slippery. Hates to be in the squad room. Prefers to be on the street. What was she doing before she left?"

"I put her on the case files to review." He knocked on Hastings' desk. "Whenever she decides to show up, let her know I need to talk to her." He shook his head and headed back to the War Room. "I'm regretting this already."

Collins stopped a few houses up the road from the address Geez provided. She looked around at her surroundings. Half the houses, if not more, were abandoned and falling apart.

She got out of her car and quietly closed the door. She checked that her service revolver was loaded and walked up to the house. Compared to the rest of the neighbourhood, the house wasn't in bad shape. But the steps up to the porch looked sketchy so she walked up the edge, along the beam. A row of potted plants hung from the top of the porch, dying plants drooping over the edge of the pots.

She held her revolver in one hand and knocked on the front door. "Police. I need to talk to the owner of the black El Camino." She waited for a minute with no response. She knocked again. "Hello?"

She lifted the welcome mat and ran her hand across the top of the door. "Where would I hide a key?" She looked around at possible hiding places, then reached up and felt in the hanging potted plant. "Bingo." She unlocked the door and pocketed the key.

She took a step into the foyer. "The is the police. The door was open. Is everything okay?" She waited for a minute, then took her revolver in both hands and stepped all the way into the house. She wrinkled her nose. A rat scurried across her path and down the hallway to the kitchen. "Lovely."

She followed the rat into the kitchen. She took in the seventies styles and grunted. "Looks like nobody has lived here in decades. A fixer-upper, I think they'd call it."

She moved down the hallway past two bedrooms and reached a closed door. She stood with her back to the wall and knocked. "Police. Anybody in there? I just want to talk." She listened for a second, then tried the knob.

The door opened into a small dark garage. She flicked on her small flashlight and shone the light into the dark. "No car. Fucking Geezer."

She found a light switch on the wall and flipped it a couple of times with no result. She stepped into the garage, playing the flashlight around the walls. Cheap shelving lined the far wall.

She shone her light below the shelving and saw a barely noticeable crack in the floor. She crouched down and followed the line, perfectly straight, the length of the garage.

She stood and bumped into one of the sections of shelving, lifting it about two inches. A *click*, followed by a deep rumbling preceded the floor slowly dropping. "Jesus. What the hell?"

She spread her feet for balance and rode the floor down. When she was about waist-deep in garage, a light came on below her. An expansive cavern spread out under the property.

A black El Camino sat right in front of her.

"Sorry, Geezer. I guess you were right," she muttered under her breath. She approached the car from the rear, revolver poised. She bent to look into the interior. Empty. She walked around to the front of the car and rested her hand on the hood. "Warm. Where are you, bitch?"

She walked around to the far side of the car. A large tarp was rolled up and placed against the wall. Her Beretta and suppressor sat on top. "Son of a bitch." She holstered her service revolver and picked up the Beretta. She hefted it, smiled and dropped it in her right side jacket pocket. She dropped the suppressor in the left. "Whole, again."

She walked to center of the space and slowly turned. Directly in front of the car stood a bank of cabinets. To the right was a table and a couple of chairs. A bar fridge was against one side of the space and a twin-sized cot was near the entrance. The space below the house was at least twice as large as the house above it. Something was providing power. Fresh air was coming from somewhere and there was ample light.

But there was nowhere to hide and the woman wasn't here.

She looked around. "How do I get the fuck out of here?"

The back wall of the closet upstairs slid down and the glass dome raised off of the chair. The Woman stepped out, took a deep breath and walked out of the bedroom and into the hall. The door to the garage was open, light from the underground space spilling out. "Oh, shit."

She stepped forward and peered into the space. She looked down on Detective Collins as she walked around, poking at shelving and tipping books in the bookcase.

"The big red button, you moron," whispered the Woman.

Almost as if on cue, Collins hit the button on the wall closest to the entrance to the cavern and the garage floor started rising. The Woman stepped back into the bedroom, ducked into the closet and tripped the hidden wall.

Collins stood on the floor as it rose. At the halfway mark the lights went out. She turned on her flashlight and watched as the false floor rose into place. "Amazing."

She left the garage, took a quick look down the hall and went out the front door.

Collins got in her car and took the ankle holster out of the glove box. She strapped it to her ankle and slid in the Beretta. She took the suppressor out of her jacket pocket and hefted it.

She dropped it back into her jacket pocket and started the car. Before she could put it into gear the garage door started opening. She turned off the ignition and slid down in her seat.

The garage door reached the top and the El Camino backed out.

"Well fuck me. Where in the fuck were you hiding?"

The car stopped on the drive until the garage door

closed, then rolled back onto the street. It pulled away and Collins started her car. "What are you up to now?

Chapter 25

The El Camino accelerated down the street. Collins floored her police car and gained. She saw the woman look in the review mirror and the El Camino surged ahead. It took a hard right hand turn, the back tires losing traction. The driver corrected and accelerated.

"Son of a bitch." Collins floored it. The El Camino skidded around another corner, Collins tight on its tail. Her phone rang as she corrected for the drift. She dug it out of her pocket. 'Unknown Number' was on the display.

"Who is this?" Collins put her phone on speaker.

"I know exactly how you feel," said the Woman. "But you've got to give me a day or so before we meet." The El Camino jumped the curb as she pulled a hard right.

"Pull over, bitch. You're dangerous. You're going to kill someone. Oh, wait. You already have."

"I can drive just as well as you can. You'll need to wait. And when we meet, you'll understand."

Collins accelerated and hit the lights and siren. "What are we waiting for? Now's as good a time as any. Pull over." Collins dumped the call and tried to pull past the El Camino.

Wilson knocked on Hastings desk. "Where is she?"

"I'm not her keeper. I'm sure there's a reason for her not being here. She's very much a lone wolf. Wolf-ess? Whatever a female wolf is called,"

"A bitch."

"Oh, please let me know when you're going to call her that. I'll have my phone ready to record it." Hastings leaned back in his chair. "You try calling her?"

"No, I was relying on telepathy. Of fucking course

I tried calling her."

"She'll get the message. What's the panic?"

Wilson sat in the chair across from the Detective. "Run through this with me. She finds half a dozen cases that are linked."

"She found four."

Wilson shrugged. "Okay, four." He wiped the corners of his mouth. "Then a scumbag she put away is released, and she's present when the serial killer offs him. It looks like that serial killer was going through her desk. Also accosted her outside, and even though Collins had the drop on her, she let her leave." He leaned forward. "How am I supposed to interpret that?"

"What are you saying? You think she's dirty?" Hastings stood. "Get the fuck back in that room. Come near me again and I might pop you."

Wilson looked up at him. "Give me another explanation that fits. Any. I don't care how ridiculous it sounds." He folded his fingers across his stomach.

"I'm waiting."

Hastings shook his head. "Get out of here."

Wilson stood. "She may have a perfectly excellent explanation. I need to hear it. See if you can get her in here, okay? You think you're such a good friend? Now's the time to demonstrate it."

She was almost alongside the El Camino when her phone rang again. She put it on speaker and slowed, pulling back behind her prey. "Hello, Hastings. What can I do for you?"

"You went out for a cigarette almost two hours ago. You're not going to have any lungs left. Wilson is looking for you. He needs to talk to you about the woman who attacked you."

"I'm sure Barnes would like to have a word too." She ran a red light in pursuit. "I'll be back at the station in less than an hour."

"I don't think that's gonna cut it. He's convinced that you have a link to this killer."

"That's insane."

"Maybe. Wilson thinks she's trying to recruit you to take over."

"Okay, *that's* insane."

"Whatever you're doing, get your bony ass in here."

"I'm kinda busy right now." She swerved to miss a dog running across the street. "I'll give you a call back in a bit."

"Busy doing what?"

"Pursuing a felon." She dumped Hastings' call and pulled a hard right into a cul-de-sac. The El Camino was parked across the road.

Collins slammed on the brakes and slid to a stop. She lifted her leg up on the seat and slid the Beretta out while keeping eyes on her target. "There's no way out of here, honey."

She screwed the suppressor on the barrel and cracked open her car door. The El Camino was on the far side of her car. The driver's door was closest to her. She crouched and ran to the front of her car, keeping her eyes on the other El Camino. The Woman glanced at her briefly, then ducked down. The passenger's side door opened.

"Oh, no you don't." Collins sprinted toward the El Camino, running around the back of the black car. The woman was crawling out of the car, almost all the way out. Collins held the silenced Beretta pointing to the ground.

"Hands out where I can see them. Now."

The woman crawled forward on her hands and knees.

"NOW."

The Woman hung her head and sighed. "I told you to leave it. Why couldn't you just leave it? Jesus, Deb, you never listen."

"Flat on the ground, hands behind your head."

She shook her head. "I can't do that. Not now. Not here. Not this way." She slid her right hand into her jacket pocket.

"I SAID HANDS. NOW."

The Woman chuckled. "Not that big on patience, are we?" She dropped to her left and pulled out the Taser and fired just as Collins shot at her.

The slug from the Beretta splintered a tree behind the Woman. She ducked the flying wood chips and continued holding the trigger on the Taser.

The barbs hit Collins in the stomach. Her back arched and she bounced her head off the side of the car as she hit the pavement.

"Really sorry I had to do that again. No choice."

Collins eyes rolled back in her head. Her jaw muscles were tight. Foam speckled her lips.

The Woman collected the wires and barbs and slammed the passenger door shut. She ran around to the other side of her car.

Collins tried to ride out the spasms, forcing her muscles to relax. Sirens sounded in the distance. She looked down at the gun still gripped in her hand.

"Oh, fuck."

She rolled over onto her hands and knees as the El

Camino roared away, bouncing over the curb and past Collins' car. She crawled across the pavement and struggled to open her car door. She dragged herself upright, put her Beretta and silencer in the glove box, closed the glove box, and dropped to the ground.

The sirens increased in volume as Collins slowly blacked out.

Chapter 26

Hastings pulled into the cul-de-sac and turned off his lights and sirens. Collins' car was sideways in the street, blocking access. Residents on their front lawns enjoyed the spectacle.

Hastings jumped out of his car, his gun drawn. "Collins, where are you?" He ran around the back of her car and saw her crumpled against the back fender. "Oh, Jesus, granny." He crouched down beside her and checked her pulse.

He grabbed his radio. "Dispatch, Officer down. We need an ambulance at," he looked at the signs and gave them the cross streets.

Collins stirred and tried to sit up.

"Hang on. Stay there. Get your bearings. Are you

hurt?"

She lifted her shirt up and looked at the marks on her stomach. The jacket wasn't there to protect her this time. The marks were an angry red. "A little."

"Jesus. Her again?"

Collins nodded and slowly sat up. "I had her this time, but she's fucking fast with that thing."

"Decades of practice."

Collins looked at him. "Right. Maybe she *is* related to the guy who invented them." She winced as she stood. "Feels like I might have bruised my bony ass, too. But I'm not going to show you that."

"Sit in my car while I canvas the citizens." A siren whooped and Hastings looked over the top of Collins' car. "Never mind. Crime scene guys are here. They can start the canvas. You can tell me what the hell happened."

Collins walked to Hastings car and sat in the passenger's seat, feet on the ground. She took a breath and scrubbed her face. "Where to start?"

Hastings crouched to get eye-to-eye with Collins. "There are people who think that you're either working with the serial killer, or she's trying to recruit you to take over. You know that. So I suggest you start from page one."

"The woman doing this flies a 60's black El Camino. I saw it behind the pool hall where Wheeler was killed. Where *she* killed Wheeler. That's a pretty rare car. Or truck. Or whatever the fuck it is. I got my CIs looking for it." She rolled her neck muscles. "I think I twisted something when I fell."

"An ambulance is coming."

"Fuck, no. I don't need an ambulance. Hot shower and some aloe on the burns and I'll be fine. Where was I?" She watched a crime scene tech remove a slug from the tree.

"The car."

"Right. One of my CIs gave me an address where he saw the car. I got the text while I was having a smoke. I took off over there."

"We'll need that address."

Collins nodded. "Sure. Whatever." She took a deep breath. "On the way there I saw the car leaving a garage." She swallowed. "Different address. I followed. After a block she must have made me. She took off, I chased her for about three miles until she fucked up and turned into this cul-de-sac."

"License plate number?"

"Didn't get it."

"You chased her for three miles and you didn't get it?"

"I was paying attention to the road." She hugged herself. "I'm cold. Can you grab my jacket out of my car?"

"Don't go anywhere."

Hastings left to get the jacket and Collins took out her phone, found the message from Geezer with the El Camino's address and deleted it. She pocketed her phone and stood to take the jacket from Hastings.

"Thanks." She stood and pulled on the jacket, snugging it around her. "I'm freezing. You cold?"

Hastings pointed at the tech removing the slug from the tree. "What did you do that to the tree for? It look at you funny?"

"Wasn't me. Last I remember is that she Tased me. Someone must have called 9-1-1 after I passed out. Next thing I know, you're leaning over me like you wanted to give me the kiss of life."

Hastings shook his head and wrote stuff in his notebook. "What's she look like?"

Collins shrugged and rubbed her face. She tried to stand and Hastings pushed her back in the seat. "Hey. Take it easy, kiddo. You grabbed one of my boobs." She looked up at Hastings. "I don't have any more than when she was in the back alley. Female, small, like my size. White, dark brown hair. Longish."

Hastings flipped his book closed. "You've got a homicidal woman stalking you and you have no idea who it is?"

Collins shook her head and stood, pushing Hasting's hand away. She held her hand to her stomach and walked away from him. "I've got to get these burns checked out. I'll talk to you later."

Hastings grabbed her by the arm. "You've got to get back to the station. The task force, as a whole, is going to want to talk to you about this."

She turned and lifted her shirt. "You want these to get infected? I've got to get some treatment."

"The ambulance is on the way."

"And the check is in the mail, and I'm from the government and here to help you. I can go get these fixed up and be back here before the ambulance shows."

Hastings looked at his watch. "Get the burns patched up and get back to the station by three."

Collins dropped her shirt, nodded and got in her car. She drove out of the cul-de-sac with her phone to her head.

"You get that number for me yet?"

"This is the IT Tech department. Who is this?"

"Detective Collins. I sent you an email with the parameters of a call to my mobile. I need to know the number that called me. It came up as blocked."

"Okay, Detective. I got it. I sent you an email about an hour ago."

"I'm in the field. Send it to my mobile right now. It's important."

She hung up, navigated a couple of blocks from the scene and waited for the message.

Hastings watched her drive away and made his own phone call. "Wilson, did we get video from behind the pool hall?"

"Such as it was. Can't tell what the woman looked like. Collins was in a bit of a shadow. It looks like she's got a weapon in her hand, but it could just as easily be her phone. The story played out pretty much as she described it."

"There was a black El Camino leaving when I

arrived. It had Wheeler's body in the back. Go over the vision again and see if you can tags off it. Anything that will help us find it. Thanks."

He hung up and looked around at the houses in the neighborhood. "Which of you suburban friends has a security system that includes video, I wonder."

Collins looked at the message on her phone, thought for a second, then dialed. It was answered after one ring.

"Is this Detective Collins?"

Collins clenched her jaw. "Who in the hell are you?"

"The question of the hour, Detective. I was wondering how this would feel, and I've got to say, it's a little bit on the strange side. Keep investigating like I know you will. It'll click, and when it does, call me again."

The Woman hung up.

Collins called back, but it went straight to generic

voicemail. "What the ever-lovin' fuck."

She tossed the phone on the seat and spat out her window. "I fucking hate riddles."

Chapter 27

Hastings walked over to the tech working the tree. "How's it going?"

"Good timing." She finished fishing the slug out of the tree and dropped in a glassine evidence bag. "It's a .32 caliber."

Hastings held up the bag and looked at the slug. "Good work. This goes to the FBI. The serial case." He swept his hand around the area. "Everything you pick up here, to the task force. Got it?"

"Absolutely, sir."

"Great." Hastings looked at the citizens watching the show. He flipped open his notebook and made his way to the closest. "Good afternoon. My name is

Detective Hastings." He flashed his credentials. "I was wondering if you could tell me what you saw today."

Collins hopped off the examination table and buttoned her blouse. "Thanks doc. I could have done that myself."

The doctor shrugged. "Probably. But at least now you know it was done right. Change those pads twice a day." She pressed a tube of antiseptic cream in Collins' hand. "Keep them clean, too."

Collins nodded and finished buttoning her top. "Absolutely. Send the bill to the station."

She walked out of the Emergency Department and dug her phone out of her jacket pocket. "Geezer, I need you, man."

"Collins? You're too old for me. But I'm flattered. Where's my fucking money?"

"Where are you?"

"Bowling alley on Central."

"I'll be there in fifteen. I'll have your money. And maybe a bit more." Collins hopped in her car. "Stay there."

Hastings stood on the last front porch and flipped his book shut. He walked down the front steps and looked up at the gable by the driveway. A half-globe security camera surveyed the neighborhood.

He turned back to the porch. "Excuse me, one more thing." He pointed at the camera. "Is that thing on?"

The father nodded. "Wouldn't be any point in having it if it wasn't."

"Would you have any problem sending me a copy of the video that shows what happened here?"

"No problem at all. Why would I have a problem?"

Hastings smiled. "Some people feel that a warrant is required to surrender information to the police. I could get one, but that would take time."

"Nah, it's all fine. How do you want it?"

Hastings took a card out of his wallet. "Can you

email it to me?"

"I'll get it to you. It'll be in an hour or so, okay?"

Hastings nodded. "No problem. Much appreciated."

Collins stepped into the disco-themed bowling alley and grimaced as a flood of memories from the 80s washed over her. "Oh, Jesus." Patti LaBelle was belting out the only French every 80's American kid knew. She squinted as mirrors on the rotating ball reflected lights in her eyes.

"Geezer, where the hell are you?" She walked past the shoe rental counter toward a raucous crowd at the far end of the alley. Geezer's follow-through as he delivered the ball reminded her of a flamingo trying to play soccer. All skinny limbs and awkward angles. He guttered the ball to the hoots and jeers of his friends. He saw Collins when he turned back to sit. She nodded him over.

"Hey, Detective. You didn't see that, did you?"

Collins fished bills out of her pocket and handed

him $300, and held another $100 in front of him. "Got something for you."

Geez looked down at her, then at the money in his hand. "Hell ya. What do you want me to do for you?"

"I'm getting a crick in my neck." She sat at a table and moved the laminated menu out of the way. "Sit."

Geez folded himself into the chair opposite. "Sat. Be fast. I'm up soon."

She spread the hundred-dollar bill flat on the table. "For you, if you can find the El Camino woman, and keep her in one place. Find her, call me and keep her from going anywhere."

Geezer looked at the money, then at Collins. "Two hundred."

"One fifty."

"Done."

Collins slide the hundred across the table. "I'll give you the other fifty when you find her. Be careful, she's got a gun."

"No, no. Hang on a second. You didn't say anything

about a gun."

Collins smiled at the tall, skinny kid. "She's not going to shoot you. She only shoots felons who have, somehow, escaped justice." She leaned forward. "That's not you, is it?"

Geezer slid the bill back across the table. "I'm not comfortable with this. Finding, sure. Holding? No way. Not when guns are involved."

Collins sucked air through her teeth and shook her head. "Kids these days. No backbone." She thought for a second, then nodded. "Okay." She slid the hundred back. "Just find her. And call me *as soon* as you see the car. You know what it looks like now. It should be faster, right?"

Geezer folded the bill and slid it into his wallet. "Any time?"

"Any time."

Hastings walked into the War Room, looked around and motioned for Wilson to follow him to a quiet corner.

"Have you heard from Collins yet," asked Hastings.

"She still works here? I haven't seen her in a long time."

"You know, older woman, small. Found the connection in the cold cases."

Wilson laughed. "Senility hasn't kicked in yet, Hastings. I need to talk to her."

"I sent her off to the hospital to get her Taser burns patched up. It shouldn't have taken this long." Hastings looked at the board. He walked over and removed a couple of pictures. "They looked extraordinarily similar to these."

Wilson shook his head and laughed. "There's no way somebody killed in the seventies or eighties was Tased. Not even remotely possible."

Hastings chewed at the inside of his lip. "Yeah, well it's something. Damned if I know what." He patted Wilson on the shoulder and handed back the photos. "I'll tell her to stop in whenever she shows."

A few hours later Collins walked in, head high, taking her jacket off as she entered. "Still shit out there. I'm over winter." She tapped on Hastings' desk. "What's new?"

"You. You're new. How's the stomach?"

Collins lifted her shirt and showed him the pair of small bandages. "I'll live."

"To a ripe old age. Follow me." Hastings led Collins into the War Room and planted her in front of Wilson.

"Wilson, this is Collins. Collins, Wilson."

"Smart ass," said Collins. "What can I do for you?"

Wilson held up a file. "The slug pulled from the tree was a thirty-two. You carry a thirty-eight? Right?"

"Yeah. Department issue."

Wilson nodded. "We're running ballistics on the slug against the older cases. Not much there, but it's worth a look." He stood and led her and Hastings to a small conference room. "So, Collins, tell me everything you can about this mysterious stalker woman.”

An hour of give and take later, looking at what little information she had from every angle Wilson could think of, Collins and Hastings left the War Room. She stopped at his desk. “So how much ballistics evidence was there?”

“From four of the victims. Plus the slug pulled from the tree.”

Collins nodded and stood there in thought.

“What are you thinking?”

“It's *got* to be somebody connected to the DA's office, maybe law enforcement.”

Hastings leaned back in his chair. “Makes sense.”

She nodded. “Everybody up in that board is a dirt bag who has, for one reason or another, dodged doing time for a crime they were clearly guilty of.”

“But there are dozens, maybe even hundreds of assholes who fit that profile over the last thirty years. And they're all still alive. How do you figure that?”

Collins dropped into her chair. "Got me. Maybe the killer didn't have the opportunity to kill those ones." She smiled. "Pity."

"Can't argue with that." Hastings looked past Collins. "Wilson is flagging us. We're needed in the War Room."

Chapter 28

Wilson stood in front of the crime board with a handful of photos from the medical examiner's office. He looked up as Collins and Hastings walked in. "Hey."

He arranged torso shots below their respective headshots. All of the torso shots had burn marks on them, consistent with Taser burns.

Collins pushed forward and took one of the photos down. She held it up in front of Wilson's face. "So you believe me now?"

"They are burns that are consistent across all of the cases. Tasers? Not likely. But they are burns consistent across all of the cases." Wilson stuck the final picture up on the board, took the one from

Collins and replaced it on the board.

He sat on the edge of a desk and crossed his arms. "Okay. We've looked at the video of the time the woman attacked you behind the station." He cocked an eyebrow at Collins. "And the video from the CCTV behind the bar." He shrugged.

"Not much, right," said Collins.

Hastings grimaced. "Not much more than squat."

Wilson held up an index finger. "Not completely nothing, though. We know the woman drives a very nice El Camino. It looked in mint condition."

Hastings nodded. "Shouldn't be too hard to find. I'll get black and whites looking for it. Something as old as that car, in the condition it's in, should be easy to find."

Collins crossed her arms and looked between Wilson and Hastings. She opened her mouth to speak, then closed it. She walked back to her desk and sat, concern etching her face.

Chapter 29

Collins tossed a file onto her desk. "Twenty-seven."

Hastings looked over at her. "Twenty-seven what?"

"El Caminos. Twenty-seven 1967 El Caminos have been reported stolen and not recovered over the last thirty years." She finger-combed her hair back and took a deep breath. "This is going to take a while. And it's late. I'll hit this in the morning." She grabbed her jacket off the back of her chair. "I'm outta here."

Wilson held his hand over the phone's mouthpiece. "Hang on a tick. Ballistics is on its way."

"I'm beat. I'll catch up tomorrow. I don't want to wait. It's been a long, long day."

A mail clerk poked his head in the War Room. "Special Agent Wilson?"

"Over here." Wilson took the envelope from the clerk and spread the contents over the evidence table in the middle of the room. Striations from every slug found in the case, including the one extracted from the tree were displayed in high-resolution photographs. The report of the findings was eight pages long.

Collins took a quick look at the photos, then grabbed the report. She skimmed the preliminaries and flipped through the pages to the conclusion. "Huh."

Wilson and Hastings held photos and examined the striations, holding pairs of photos beside each other, comparing markings on the slugs.

Hastings put his pair down and looked over Collins' shoulder. "What?"

"They all match. Including the one from the tree."

"As expected." Wilson dropped the photos on the table and grabbed his phone. "I've got to amp up the search for this car. Collins, give me the list of stolen cars. I'll get uniforms to visit the original owners."

Collins handed the list to Wilson. "The slug from the tree matched, too? So it's definitely her."

Wilson lowered the handset, mid-dial. "I'm surprised that you're surprised. It was expected. And now we have a solid identification of the killer."

Collins raised her eyebrows. "Solid identification? It's a mystery woman in a car we can't find. Doesn't sound solid to me."

Wilson looked at Hastings, then at Collins. "You don't look convinced. Hastings, she doesn't look convinced. This is ballistics, Collins. Ballistics have a tendency to *not* lie."

"No, I'm convinced. Great break. Get a platoon of guys out looking for her, and we'll have this case closed in no time." She pulled her jacket tight. "So you don't need me around here. I'll see you tomorrow."

Chapter 30

Collins walked out of the station into a cold drizzle. She wrapped her jacket around herself and hunched into the cold. She ran across the street to the parking lot and climbed into her car. She started the engine and punched the dashboard.

"Fucking ballistics. What in the hell is going on? How is that even possible?" She dug out her phone, searched for the text from the IT tech and called the woman.

"Detective."

"What do I call you? Bitch?"

"That's not very nice, Detective. Call me Jane, if you want. Jane Doe."

"We usually reserve that name for unidentified dead

bodies. Are you volunteering?"

The Woman laughed. "I'm not ready for that quite yet. Soon, maybe. Job's not finished yet."

Collins took a deep breath. "You think you're pretty smart, but you can't be that smart, taking my calls, talking as long as you are."

"Oh, you can trace it if you want. It won't make any difference. I won't be here when you get here. Toodles, Detective. Don't worry. I won't be killing anyone tonight. Promise."

The call dropped. "That's nice." She tossed the phone on the passenger's seat and pulled out of the parking lot. Her phone started ringing. She picked it up, looked at the display—Hastings—and tossed it back on the seat. "I don't feel like talking until I figure out what the hell."

Collins drove aimlessly, intermittent wipers keeping the windshield clean. She ended up at the cemetery on Mt. Elliot Street.

The wind off Lake Erie whipped through the trees,

amplifying the cold. She leaned on her car, parked under a leafless elm, and shivered. It had been a while. She pulled on her gloves, got out, and closed the door.

Her leather-soled shoes squeaked on the damp concrete. She hunched into her jacket, trying to keep as much warmth in her body as possible. Her eyes watered. She wiped them with her sleeve and sniffled. A passerby could be excused for thinking she was crying. She wasn't, and she wouldn't.

She leaned into the hill, one foot trudging after another. Her nose was cold, and her cheeks were stiff. The walk was automatic. She could have passed a flaming elephant, and she wouldn't have noticed. Thoughts were tumbling through her head, and she found it difficult to grab any individual one. They clashed and collided and made very little sense. She needed clarity. A chat with Larry might get her that.

She came over the crest of the hill and saw her destination. The bench was covered in rain; the concrete would be freezing.

She used her sleeve to wipe away the wet on the seat in front of her husband's headstone. "It's been too long, Larry. Still miss you. Still pissed off at you for dying the way you did. Wasn't fair."

She took a deep breath and leaned back. "I'm fine. Thanks for asking. Except some really weird shit is coming down, and I don't know what to make of it. You were always the smart one. Maybe you can help me. Give a sign, big guy. How do I deal with the crazy bitch?"

She sat forward, leaned her arms on her legs and interlaced her fingers. "I can't figure it out. She's too good, one step in front of me all the time. Disappearing like a wraith, then appearing when I least expect her." She shook her head. "If anything comes to you, let me know."

She stood and rested her hand on his headstone. "One of these days I'll visit in person, big guy. Until then, keep a place warm for me. I'm tired of this fucking cold."

She gave the headstone a pat. "Until next time. I promise it'll be sooner."

She shoved her gloved hands in her jacket pockets and walked back to her car. She wasn't any further ahead in her understanding, but the talk made her feel better.

Hastings hung up his phone and looked across his desk at Wilson. "Still no answer."

"This doesn't look good for your friend." Wilson crossed his legs. "I'm not sure what to make of it, but she's not being very smart. Track her phone. Find her."

The rain poured from the sky now, and Collins' wipers beat double-time trying to keep the screen clear. She pulled up in front of the woman's house. "Where are you, crazy bitch?"

She grabbed the Beretta and silencer from the glove box and got out in the rain. She flipped the hood up on her jacket and stepped onto the porch. She unlocked the front door and pushed it open, swiftly clearing the rooms—empty.

She pulled off the hood, opened the door to the garage, walked across to the shelving and gave it a bang. The floor started lowering.

She extended the Beretta and squatted, sweeping the cavernous area below the property. She stood slowly as the garage floor lowered until it reached the bottom. She swept with the gun, left to right. The room was empty.

"Dammit." She smacked the button on the wall and rode the floor back up. "This is getting on my fucking nerves."

She walked back out into the rain, gun by her side, rain pounding down on her head. She looked up at the sky, raindrops peppering her face. "Just beautiful."

She got in her car and turned the heat and fan on to clear the window. The Beretta and silencer went into the glove box. Her phone was still on the passenger seat. Five missed calls from Hastings.

"It just gets better." She punched the number. "What?"

"Finally, Collins. I was just leaving so good timing."

"For you, maybe. Why have you been calling?"

"I'm—we're—trying to find you. I called your apartment half a dozen times, too, so you can disregard any messages you have there from me. You're chasing that woman, aren't you?"

"Just driving around. Trying to wind down."

"I think that's bullshit. It's turning into crap out there. That rain is going to freeze tonight. Are you okay?"

"I'm fine. I'll see you tomorrow." She hung up her phone and dropped it on the seat.

Hastings looked at his phone and pulled on his jacket. "Hey, Wilson. I just talked to her. She's fine. Was just driving around. Unwinding." He walked into the War

Room and sat beside Wilson. "She sounded pretty tired."

Wilson had his head down reading a file. He finished a section, then looked up. "Where's Collins? You get the trace back?"

"I just told you. I was talking to her. She was driving around clearing her head."

Wilson held up a sheet of paper. "She's going to sit out for a few days while we investigate this. Administrative leave. Paid."

Hastings nodded. "Not a bad idea. She sounded shaken. Plus those burns on her stomach have to sting."

Wilson waved that away and shook his head. "No, her report from the attack at the cul-de-sac doesn't scan."

Hastings took the paper from him. "Where?"

"That shot to the tree. The way she described it, the woman took that shot. But based on witness statements and the physical layout, that mystery woman couldn't have. Until we get to the bottom of this I want Collins off the street."

Hastings took out his notebook and compared his notes against the report. He flipped the pages and went back and forth then dropped the report on Wilson's desk. "She was rattled. I'll let Barnes know."

"No, you go. I'll tell him. See you tomorrow."

Hastings nodded. "Okay. Tomorrow." He flipped the collar of his jacket up and walked into the rain. He opened his phone and called Collins.

"I thought we talked all we had to today, Hastings."

He got in his car and started the engine. "Don't bother coming in for the next couple of days."

"Something I said?"

"The very Special Agent is having difficulties reconciling your report with witness statements and crime scene tech reports. He wants you out of the frame until he sorts it out."

"Jesus, Hastings, I was shaken up. That Taser jolt must have scrambled my neurons."

"Yeah, I'm sure he'll come to the same conclusion. Take a couple of paid days off."

Collins sat at the curb in front of her apartment, wipers flogging the rain. "Yeah, okay. I'll talk to you later."

She terminated the call and slid the phone in her pocket. "Goddamned tree." She got out of the car and rushed through the rain to the apartment. She shook herself off and entered the building.

Half a block away the Woman sat in her black El Camino, watching.

Chapter 31

Barnes stormed into the War Room with a piece of paper in his hand. "Where in the fuck is Wilson?"

Wilson stood and motioned Barnes over to his desk. "What's up, Captain?"

"Agent Wilson, what in the hell are you doing with Collins?"

Wilson scratched the stubble on his jaw. "It's kinda awkward, Cap, and I'm hoping that I'm wrong, but there's a lot of evidence that doesn't look good for her." He held up his hands, stopping Barnes from interrupting. "I know, Collins has an excellent pedigree. But it doesn't scan for me. I've benched her, as you put it, for a couple of days while we investigate this further."

Barnes held Wilsons gaze for a couple of seconds. "Send me a copy of this evidence that concerns you. I'm going to put it down as a personal break." He wiped at the corners of his mouth. "Actually, get that evidence and follow me to my office and explain to me what it is that doesn't track."

Collins padded into her kitchen in a bathrobe and slippers. She filled her kettle with water and plugged it in. She took her phone out of her robe pocket and considered it for a moment. Leaned on the counter and dialed.

"Collins? I thought you'd be sleeping in," said Hastings.

"Can't. Body won't let me. Too many years on this job." She unplugged the kettle and poured water into her cup of instant coffee grounds. "I've got a huge favor to ask."

"Anything, for you."

"Can you get a copy of all the ballistics evidence

and send it to me? Something about that report isn't sitting right."

"Is this about the tree slug? Ballistics doesn't lie, Collins. And look at the striations. Don't need a computer to tell you the slugs all came from the same barrel."

"I know, I know. Still, my gut is telling me something's off."

"Tell me. I'll have a look at it."

"Nah, you've got enough on your plate managing the feds. And it's nothing I can put my finger on. I know I'm on administrative leave, or whatever the hell Barnes is calling it, but it'll keep my mind active." Collins spooned some sugar into the cup and stirred.

"Beat's watching daytime TV, I guess. I suppose it can't cause any harm. I'll messenger the copies over. Give me an hour or so."

"I owe you, kiddo. Probably best if Wilson doesn't find out. I don't think he likes me."

"You got that right. I'll keep it quiet. Sit back and

relax. Get used to being off the job."

Collins grunted. "Thanks again." She dropped the phone back in her robe pocket and took a sip of coffee. "Oh, Jesus, that's horrible."

She shuffled into the small living room, put her coffee on the table by her chair and stretched. She opened her robe and looked at her waist. She gave it a pat, and pinched the fat above her hip. "I need to work on this. Someday. Not today."

She eased into the recliner and kicked up the footrest. "So this is retirement." She poked the remote and took a sip of coffee, wincing again at the taste. "Maybe a good coffee machine is in order."

She turned up the volume on the television and started scrolling through the channels. "Talk show. Talk show. Kid's show. Talk show. Chinese news. Korean news. French news. Fucking hell." She turned off the television and tossed the remote on the floor. "What in the hell am I going to do when I retire for real?"

Chapter 32

Collins awoke with a start. The knocking on the door continued. She wiped the drool off her chin and pushed herself out of the chair. "Hang on to your horses. I'm coming." She opened the front door to a messenger with a large envelope.

"Detective Deborah Collins?"

Collins held out her hand. "That's me. Thanks."

"I need to see some identification."

"Really? Jesus. Wait here." Collins closed the door and found her wallet. She looked around at her small, almost empty apartment and sighed. She shook her head and returned to the front door.

She opened her detective shield/photo ID and showed it to the deliveryman. "Okay? You believe it's me?"

"Sorry, ma'am. My instructions were pretty explicit." He offered a pen and clipboard. "Sign, please. Fourth row down."

Collins scribbled her signature and took the envelope. "Thanks."

She closed the door and spilled the contents onto her dining room table and spread out the photographs. She arranged them, based on the tags, chronologically.

"What am I missing here?" She read over the report carefully. The ballistics work was good. Very good. She couldn't fault the work. "Except she didn't shoot the tree. I did."

Collins rummaged through drawers in the kitchen until she found a high-power magnifying glass. She examined each photo carefully, making notes in the margins.

She moved the photo of the striations from the bullet removed from the tree to the far left. She spent the next hour carefully examining each photo, comparing finer details in the photographs and re-ordering them. She placed the last one and stood back.

The photos were arranged from tree slug, then 1977, 1986, 2002 and the Wheeler ballistics.

She looked at the photos with the glass again and swapped the 2002 and 1986 photos.

Tree slug, the 1977 murder, followed by 2002, 1986 and Wheeler, a couple of days ago.

She dropped the glass on the table and took a step back. "Son of a bitch."

Wilson hung up the phone. "Hastings, where are you with the cars?"

Hastings flipped the paper onto his desk and sat back in his chair in the War Room. "Jesus, Collins must have arranged this so she'd get suspended. Do you know how old the owners of new 1967 El Caminos are now?"

"Some forty years older than when they bought

them."

"Closer to fifty. Fuck me. Half of these people are dead and their families know nothing about the stolen car. The other half are pushing the limits of lucidity. I had one guy tell me three different stories during the course of the conversation, and I'm not convinced any of them are true. Two of them involved clowns."

"So what are you telling me?"

"I got nothing. Nothing on the car, anyway. We're not really any further ahead."

"We know who did this."

Hastings waggled his hand "We know that, yes. But we don't know who she is."

"So we find her. How hard can it be?"

"You'd think, right? Less than a million people in this city, and we're only looking for one. She's been extremely good at hiding for the last forty years." Hastings pointed at the board. "We don't even know if that's all of her victims."

Wilson unbuttoned his shirt cuffs and rolled up his

sleeves. "So what are your next steps?"

"I don't know. Collins is looking at the ballistics to see what she can tease from them."

Wilson stopped what he was doing. "What?"

"She thinks there's something wonky about them. I sent copies over this morning." Hastings winced. "Shit. She didn't want me to tell you."

Wilson laced his fingers and leaned his elbows on his desk. He rested his chin on his fingers. "What does she expect to find with ballistics? That's the most clear-cut part of the case. It confirms the linkage of most of those cases."

"All but one, actually. We found where Packer was killed and removed a slug from the dirt. Matches."

"Like I said. There's nothing new to be found there."

"So I guess there's no problem with her looking at the copies then." Hastings shrugged. "You're not pissed?"

"Would it make any difference? She's clearly

Barnes' favorite."

Hasting raised his eyebrows. "I thought I was. Are you sure?"

"Yeah, fuck off, Hastings. Work the car some more. Seems to be the only tangible thing that ties us to the killer. Get some of your CIs on the street looking for it."

Chapter 33

Collins pulled her jacket on and stabbed a speed dial on her phone. "Geezer, you got anything for me?"

Geezer sounded confused. "Did I call you, Detective?"

"Where's my car?"

"Was I supposed to be looking for your car?"

Collins got in her car and started it. "Jesus, Geez. What the hell? The El Camino. Have you found it yet?"

She pulled away from the curb, listening to silence. "Geezer?"

"Trying' ta think, Detective. I gave you that address at the house, right?"

Collins shook her head. "Keep looking, Geez. Don't

make me track you down and take my money back."

She tossed her phone in the center console and pointed her car toward the house where she saw the car the first time.

"We need her in here, Hastings. Track her down and tell her to get here as fast as she can." Wilson scribbled notes along the edge of a transcript.

"What's up? More ballistics?"

"I'm not satisfied with a number of things. I need to talk to her face to face again. Track her down."

Hastings looked at the FBI agent for a minute. "Okay. Any specific time?"

"As fast as she can. I said that already."

Hastings picked up his phone. "Right."

Collins parked a block away from the house where she first saw the El Camino. She had to start somewhere. She walked up the steps of the house beside her target and knocked on the door.

It opened a crack, security chain in place. She held her police ID up to the opening. "Hi there. I'm Detective Collins, 1st precinct. Can I ask you some questions about the house next door?"

The face withdrew and the security chain released. The door opened and an elderly man opened the door, peering out behind Collins. "Detective Collins." The man opened the door wider and smiled. Scars from decades old burns pulled at the corners of his mouth. He had scars on his neck and on his left wrist, up his arm and under his sleeve. "Please, come in."

Collins furrowed her brow. "Do I know you?"

"It's been a very long time, and I was pretty wrapped up when we last met."

Collins stood straight as recognition dawned on her. "Stew Phillips." She moved in and gave him a long hug. "Fifteen years." She wiped a tear and took a step back. "Crap. I'm sorry. How are you? Still Principal?"

Stew looked around his house and smiled. "Retired almost six years now. I'm surviving. And you are looking quite good."

"For an old girl, right?"

Stew chuckled. "Can I get you a cup of tea?"

"Oh, I'd love to sit and talk for hours, but I've got a lot to do today. I've only got a couple of questions. It won't take long."

Stewart flitted about like a happy plover. "Now that you know where I live, you must come back for a longer visit." He looked around. "Apologies for the mess."

Collins shook her head. "This place is immaculate. Please, just sit and relax."

"Shouldn't I be saying that to you?" Stewart smiled and took a seat, indicating a chair across from him for Collins.

She settled in and leaned forward. "Just a few questions about that empty house next door."

Stew cocked his head and smiled. "There may be more than a few questions, I'm afraid."

"Why's that?"

"The kids here about think the place is haunted. For decades now there'd be strange noises and lights coming from that house."

"Nobody lives there?"

Stew chuckled. "Look at the place. It's hardly ready for Better Homes." Stewart shrugged. "Given the latest economic mess, a lot of places are abandoned. The cycle will swing back eventually, but I'm afraid this neighborhood is going to take longer than most."

"Maybe. Just so I'm clear on this: You have no idea who owns the house?"

Stew shrugged and smiled apologetically.

Collins wrote a note in her pad. "Have you ever seen a black El Camino around? Late sixties. Mint condition."

Stew smiled. "What's all this about? Should I be concerned?"

"No, Stew, I don't think so. You haven't escaped justice recently, have you? Skipping bail?" She smiled and closed the file

Stewart frowned. "No. I've never even received a parking ticket. Why?"

Collins smiled and stood. "Nothing. Don't worry about it. Thanks for your hospitality." She pressed a card into his hand. "Give me a call, okay? I'll buy you coffee. We'll catch up."

Stewart showed her to the door. "Absolutely. No problem." He watched through the front door window as she crossed the street. He looked at the house next door and smiled.

Collins hit a few other houses around her target with similar results. Everyone thought the house was abandoned. Nobody knew nuttin'.

Collins walked back to her car and dropped the file on the seat. She looked up the block at the house for a second, then removed the Beretta from the glove box. She attached the suppressor and walked up the street.

She checked for an audience, then walked up the front steps. Knowing the canvas that she just did, she was sure people were watching. Nothing could be done about that.

She paused briefly at the front door, then unlocked it and pushed it open, gun in her outstretched hands. "Come out, come out, wherever you are."

She swept through the house a little faster than her first visit. She took quick looks in the kitchen and the two bedrooms, satisfying herself that the house was empty, and headed to the garage.

She knocked the shelf and rode the floor down to the lower level. The space was empty. She looked around, tapping her gun against her leg.

She stepped off the lowered floor and poked the rolled up tarp. Next to the card table was a small desk with two monitors on it. They looked like nothing she'd seen before. They were almost paper thin and translucent. A keyboard sat between them. She tapped the space bar with no result.

She turned back to the small kitchen area. One of the cupboard doors was half open. She pushed it the rest of the way open with the silencer on her gun. Long-life juice packs and milk stood among vacuum-sealed packets of biscuits and tins of fruit, all of them dating from the late-90s.

"Huh." She slammed the cupboard shut and holstered her gun. She hit the button on the wall and rose back into the garage. She used her flashlight and examined every corner of the dark space. "Where is it?" She made the rounds around the garage twice, finally conceding that what she was looking for wasn't there.

"It needs some space, wherever it is."

She walked through the house, this time spending far more time inspecting every corner. She looked for walls that were too thick for conventional design.

She glanced in the bathroom - too small for even a bathroom - and walked past into the first bedroom. The carpet was worn and the wallpaper was fading. A closet door stood ajar. She walked into the room and took a quick look and shook her head.

She abandoned that room and moved into the other bedroom. It was larger than the first, with a large closet taking up a corner. The carpet was as worn as in the other room.

She was turning to leave when something caught her eye. She squatted down and looked at the carpet from an angle. It showed a faint indication of foot traffic from the bedroom door to the closet.

She stood slowly and removed her Beretta from her ankle holster. She spun on the suppressor and took slow, quiet steps to the closet door. She paused, settled herself, and then yanked the door open.

It was empty. A wooden hanger bar spanned the width, supporting three metal hangers. She reached to move the hangers when her phone rang, startling her.

"Jesus." She took a deep breath and looked at the name on the phone. "What is it, Hastings?"

"You home?"

Collins looked around the bedroom. "Yes. No. Not home. On an errand. Why?"

"Where are you?"

"What does it matter? I'm not in the office. That's what's important, right?"

"Barnes wants you to come in to go over your statement again. Reconciling it with some of the witness statements. It's just that some of the discrepancies don't make much sense."

"Witnesses are idiots. Remember?"

"Doesn't matter. Barnes wants you in here."

Collins looked at her phone, then hung up. "Shit, shit, shit."

She stepped back into the closet and grabbed the wooden pole and gave it a tug. Nothing. She slid the hangers to one side and was stopped by the last one, permanently stuck to the pole.

She squinted and cocked her head. Remembering how the shelving led to the cavern below the garage, she nudged the hanger upward. When it reached the top of its travel she heard a 'snick' and the back wall slowly dropped.

"This is nuts."

The wall sunk into the floor, exposing an overstuffed chair covered by a glass dome. She tapped on the glass with the barrel of the gun and looked around for a way to lift it. She dropped the Beretta and bent down, trying to get her fingers under the edge, to no avail.

She picked up her gun and took a step back when she heard the garage door rolling up.

Chapter 34

The Woman sat in the idling El Camino, waiting for the garage door to open far enough, then sped in, poking the garage door opener button as she did. It closed behind her, enveloping her and the car in darkness.

The car's interior light was enough for her to find the correct shelf, and after a bump, she and the car slowly lowered.

She drove the car off the pad and into the cavern. Something about the space felt off. She removed her gun from its holster and eased out of the car.

She walked slowly through the space, stopping in front of the cupboards. She cocked her head to one side and slowly closed the cupboard door with the barrel of her gun.

She walked the desk and reached behind one of the monitors and pressed a power button. Both screens lit up. The Woman typed a couple of commands, and a grid of video images appeared on both monitors. The left one showed the view outside the house from nine cameras. The right was nine videos from upstairs.

She saw Collins in the bedroom and zoomed on her face. "Took you long enough."

She spun the silencer onto the gun and stepped on the concrete pad. She bumped the button with the heel of her hand and slowly rode the floor up.

Collins stepped out of the bedroom and walked slowly to the connecting door to the garage. She listened as the floor rose into place and stood with her back to the wall, both hands on the Beretta. She readied herself and pointed the gun at the door.

"I'm pretty sure I know what you are. Come out of the garage and keep your hands where I can see them."

The door cracked open and a hand extended into the hallway holding a silenced Beretta, index finger looped in the trigger guard, gun upside down. "Hey, you. Don't shoot. I'm stepping out slowly, Detective."

The door opened a little wider and the Woman stepped into the hallway. She pulled the hood off and looked at Collins.

Collins took a step back. Standing in front of her was an older version of herself, a little more wrinkled, hair dyed brown. "Jesus." She took another step backward and stumbled, landing on her ass. Her weapon discharged, a silenced shot delivering a slug to the doorframe a few inches from Collins Older's arm.

Collins Older flinched. "Careful."

Collins blinked. "Jesus. You're going to need to explain this." She lowered her gun and slowly stood, one hand on the wall, steadying herself. She cocked her head. "I like what you did with your - our - hair." She lifted the gun again. "Explain. Or get me a drink."

Collins Older smiled. "You're taking this pretty well."

"I don't think so."

Collins Older put her gun in her pocket. "What gave me away?"

"The ballistics."

"How so?"

Collins held up her Beretta. "The slug from this gun matched the ballistics from the slugs pulled from Wheeler, for one."

"Unfortunate."

"That would have been just a strange anomaly. Maybe an error within the ballistics team. But that wasn't all of it. When I looked closely at the striations from five murders and the slug from the tree, it became evident that the killings weren't done in chronological order. The more a handgun is used, the more degraded the barrel becomes. Easy to see in the ballistics if you look closely. The slug in the tree was the oldest and the Wheeler killing was most recent.

Only one highly improbable explanation."

Collins Older chuckled. "Impressive. I don't know anyone else who would have caught that."

"You need to show me how you do it. I found the chair under the glass. I'm assuming that's the mechanism."

Collins Older leaned against the wall. "Wow. Almost thirty years of my mistakes to pass on to you."

Collins half-smiled and looked at her older self a little closer. "You're telling me you're over eighty? No way."

"Seventy-eight. We look good, don't we?" Sirens whooped as a cop car sped down the street. "Shit. Probably not us, but let's head downstairs. I've got a bottle of very old scotch down there. You look like you could use a shot." She held the door and followed Collins into the garage. "How did you find access to the bat-cave?"

Collins stood in the middle of the floor. "Bumped the shelf by mistake. Surprised nobody else has bumped into it."

"This house is haunted."

"So I've heard."

Collins Older moved the shelf and stepped onto the lowering floor. "Maybe you'll put a lock on it."

"It's not locked now, so it's unlikely I will."

Collins Older shook her head. "Time travel messes with your head. Just think of it this way: If you haven't done it yet, you won't notice a change, anywhere in your timeline. You can fold back and forth as much as you want, your actual, real life will continue to extend in a linear fashion and all the changes you see will play out the same way."

The garage floor reached the bottom and both women stepped off. Collins Older poked the button and watched the floor rise.

"So why did you kill Wheeler," asked Collins.

"Why were you behind the pool hall?" Collins Older sat at the table. She reached into the cupboard and pulled out a dusty bottle and two glasses.

Collins took her Beretta and placed it on the table and sat across from her. "Okay. Point made."

Collins Older poured two drinks and placed her Beretta on the table also. Collins picked them both up and compared them. "Same gun. Same serial number. Great minds." She put them both back down. "Wheeler couldn't have an opportunity to mess up and kill another kid. I didn't care anymore. If the courts couldn't do it, I sure as hell could."

Collins Older nodded. "I felt the same way. Wheeler wasn't *my* start though. He was *yours*. Sort of."

"Smith?"

Collins Older cocked her head. "Who?"

"Swan dive off a roof."

"Ah, yes. The guy bounced like a deflated football." She threw back her drink and wiped her mouth. "That fucker. The hatred, it doesn't fade, you know? I'd go after him today. In a heartbeat." She held her head in her hands. "I held that baby girl in my arms as she died, waiting for an ambulance. Smith was so drunk he couldn't stand. Puked all over the back seat of my car." She slapped her hands on the table. "Anywho. Smith was my trigger, and Wheeler was yours."

A distant hammering on the door filtered through to them in the cavern. Collins Older held up her hand. "Shh."

A Uniform knocked on the front door again, peering in the window as he did. "Is anybody here? Constable Harrison looking for Detective Collins." The constable knocked a third time then activated his lapel microphone. "Dispatch, this place is empty. What's the next address?"

Hastings listened to the phone, nodding, then hung up. "Cross that one off the list."

Wilson stood facing the map, his arms crossed. "Why there?"

"The techs came back with pings for her phone from

last night. Most of the time she was at the cemetery, visiting Larry, no doubt, but there was a locate in this neighborhood. The neighbors said she was asking about that house." He shrugged. "No idea why, and the place is empty. Has been for years."

Wilson didn't turn away from the map. "Keep looking."

"I'm going to go work on something else. There's a BOLO out for her. There are better things to do than chase one of our own."

Collins Older watched the images on the monitor. "They're gone."

Collins leaned back in her chair. "This is some sort of weird Back to the Future shit. You hide down here all the time?"

"Only when I'm in a time stream that's looking for me. Like this one is. I return to *my* time and I'm just a retired cop who spends the winters in Tucson and summers back here." She smiled. "Stew Phillips takes care of the place while I'm gone. Remember Stew?"

"That crazy bastard. Had me completely fooled." Collins slumped in her chair. "If that arsonist hadn't skipped, Stew wouldn't have burned. And Larry would be alive."

Collins Older laced her fingers in her lap. "Our motivation."

Chapter 35

Hastings rolled his chair back and checked his watch. "I'm outta here." He pulled his jacket off the back of his chair, looked at Collins' desk and shook his head. "I don't get you, lady." He pulled on his jacket and walked past the War Room on the way out.

Wilson looked up from his work. "Where you going, Hastings?"

"Home. It's been a long day."

The Agent shook his head and pushed himself to his feet. "We're not finished."

"I am." Hastings continued walking out of the station.

Wilson intercepted him, blocking his exit, arms crossed.

"Give me a break," said Hastings. "We're not going to duke it out, are we?"

"I get the impression that you'd defend her to the death. That she can do no wrong."

Hastings shrugged. "I've known her a lot longer than you have. A lot longer than you ever will. She's ornery, obstinate, extremely smart and has the highest closure rate in the city."

"And pissed off about having to retire because she'll have nothing. She hates the fact that Wheeler was released, and delighted that he's been picked off."

Hastings cocked his head. "Your point?"

"Prime candidate for this killer to recruit as a replacement."

Hastings shook his head and pushed past Wilson. "You're full of shit, Wilson. Find the car, find the woman and wrap this up. It's your case. I'm going home."

Collins Older handed Collins a juice pack. "Keep

hydrated."

Collins looked at the date and handed it back. "It expired fifteen years ago."

"Drink. These things are great. They last forever. If it hasn't puffed up by now, it never will."

Collins looked at the box for a second, then stabbed it with its straw. "I puke, it's on you."

Collins Older laughed. "You'll have to clean it up. I'm out of here."

"You going to show me how that thing works? And I've got a couple of questions."

Collins Older looked up. "Yeah, let's do this." She pushed the button to lower the garage floor. She rested her hand on the El Camino. "You'll have to get rid of this."

"Yeah. We all know about it. It's going to be difficult getting another one with the heat on me."

Collins Older stepped onto the garage floor. "Walk with me."

"And another gun." Collins stepped on to the floor

and her older self pushed the button. "But I don't think I'm comfortable with all this."

Collins Older squinted and took Collins' hand. "There are a certain class of people out there that don't deserve to walk among the rest of us. Most get put in jail where the natural order of things reduces their life expectancy to months, at best."

The floor reached its destination. "And there are the others."

Collins Older nodded. "Like Wheeler. And Ruiz."

Collins walked into the hallway. "But something doesn't make sense. I'm just going to be going back killing the same people you've already killed."

"No, it doesn't work like that. Different timelines. Different lives. Your future is yours. Whatever you do is unique to you."

"So why aren't you getting these guys before they do what they do?"

Collins Older shrugged apologetically. "If only. If I went back and killed Wheeler before he committed any crimes, we wouldn't know that we had to kill him. So we wouldn't go back to kill him. That's where the paradox happens. We let the system do its thing. We clean up the mess the courts don't." She smiled. "I know it would be great to take these guys off the streets before they did anything, but I can't figure out a way to do it."

"Still gotta get a car. And a gun. And pick some names."

"And, please, no Tasers. Big mistake." Collins Older walked into the closet and lowered the back wall. She pointed at the panel. "Place your palm on this."

Collins pressed her hand against it and the glass dome raised. "Okay." She looked at the keyboard on the chair. "So how does this work?"

"You enter the date and time of your destination."

"No, I know that. Who do I pick?"

"You've got computers. You can find them." She got into the chair. "I'm finished. You're up."

"No, hang on. Too many questions. Like how did you find this–this thing?"

"I was number six. How the first of us found it, I have no idea. You keep an eye on a younger version of yourself, and when you–she–starts exhibiting the same tendencies you are, recruit her." She started entering a date in the machine. "An infinite loop."

"What about a car? And a gun?"

"Really? This machine exists as far back as 1965. Go back and steal something from the impound lot and park it here. It'll be downstairs when you return. Same for the gun." She entered the last digit and pressed the ENTER key. "See ya. Be good."

The dome lowered and she slowly faded away among the electrical arcing and strong thrumming sound.

Collins stood and watched as her older version faded. "Damn. Kafka was a piker."

Chapter 36

Collins hit the station early. Off the top of her head she knew a couple of cases that qualified, and there'd be more.

She bypassed the coffee and left her jacket on as she sat in front of her computer. She closed her eyes in thought for a second, then started filtering the search query.

After a couple of false starts resulting in far too many results she narrowed the list of names down to a Baker's Dozen. She flipped open a pad of paper and started writing names, crimes and dates.

She looked up and saw Barnes and Wilson coming down the stairs from Barnes' office. "Jesus," she muttered. "What time do I have to get in to beat these guys?" She put her head down and wrote faster.

Names. Crimes. Dates.

She looked up and saw Wilson peel off into the War Room and Barnes angle toward her desk.

She ripped the page off the pad, folded it and stuffed it in her pocket. She cleared the history from the database query and closed down her screen just as Barnes reached her.

"You're here, why?"

"Hey, Cap. Just filing my expenses. I'm out of your hair effective now." She pushed back her chair. "I should be on the case. You know that. I linked most of the victims and I'm still in great shape." She patted her stomach and winced. "Okay, Sarah maybe I'll start hitting the gym."

Wilson walked out of the War Room and stopped Collins' exit. "A few minutes of your time, Detective?"

Collins looked over her shoulder at Barnes, then nodded. "What's up?"

"I'm having a hard time connecting all these dots. Come on in. Have a seat. Can I get you a coffee?"

Collins slowly eased into a chair across from the FBI agent. "No coffee, thanks. I'm not sure I can help you any more than I already have. I was Tased in that cul-de-sac and don't really remember anything."

Wilson waved that away. "Let's go back to the beginning."

Collins nodded. "Okay. Fifty-five years ago, roughly, my daddy's pee-pee got hard, and he stuck it in my mommy. Nine months later -"

"Can it, Detective. I don't have time for horseshit. When did this woman first approach you?"

Collins smiled. "Lighten up, Fibbie. The video that you've probably already analyzed every frame of, while I was trying to have a smoke break behind the station, was the first."

Wilson nodded. "When you could have apprehended her but for some reason didn't. Wheeler would still be alive right now if you'd apprehended her."

No he wouldn't, thought Collins. "Can't explain it, really. Didn't know she was our target at the time." She shrugged. "Wheeler's no loss, if you ask me."

"Be that as it may, Detective. There's no audio on the video. What did she say?"

"It was all bullshit, actually. She wanted me to can the serial case. Torpedo it. Sink it." She laughed. "Like I have that kind of weight."

"Well, we know why she'd want the case tanked. What I'm failing to understand is why you?"

"Got me, Wilson." She moved to stand. "Will that be all?"

"No. Sit. There were two other instances of you interacting with this woman, which is highly unusual."

"Hey, I only looked her up the third time, after Wheeler was killed. You want to know why she targeted me, find her and ask her. I'm retired, or close enough, so I'll leave it in your capable hands."

She stood and smoothed her jacket. "Later, Wilson. At your suggestion, I'm taking a couple of days of administrative leave. You know how to reach me." She saluted him with her index finger and walked out of the station.

Barnes walked into the War Room. "What was that about?"

Wilson tossed a whiteboard marker on his desk. "What in the hell is she up to?"

"She's a bit of a renegade. Never seemed to bother with convention. Great cop, though." Barnes pointed at the board. "How's it going here? Any movement?

Wilson slumped into his chair. "She's proving to be very elusive. Other than the ballistics, she's left nothing behind. In fact, if she hadn't approached Collins, we wouldn't even know she's a she."

Barnes chuckled. "If anyone was going to get wrapped up in this it would be Collins." He crossed his arms and sat on the corner of a desk. "So what does the ballistics tell us?"

"We tracked it to one weapon. A Beretta 92 that should have been in your evidence locker, but is missing."

"Fuck. Someone in my station?"

Wilson sighed. "Yeah, it's not that straightforward. The Beretta was used in a homicide in 2003. The first killing attributed to this serial was in 1976."

Barnes sat back. "Huh. Who was the victim in 2003? And why isn't he on the board?"

"Some sap named Hopkins. Not on the board because his killer was caught red-handed - his wife caught him with his boyfriend and wasn't that tolerant. She's been locked up since she was arrested, and will stay locked up until she dies of old age."

"There's got to be a link between her and this killer."

"I've got an agent talking to her. Or trying to. She's been uncommunicative to date. But we can't find anything linking her to these serial killings. Her husband bought the gun years ago and she *claims* it was never used."

"An enigma wrapped in a puzzle, and so on. We're positive with the ballistics?"

Wilson raised his eyebrows. "You tell me. It's your ballistics team."

Barnes opened his mouth, ready to offer some pithy response, when Hastings ran into the War Room.

"Wilson, Captain, you've got to see this."

Hastings grabbed a keyboard, typed a couple of commands and pointed to a large monitor behind Wilson's head.

Wilson pivoted in his seat. "What is this?"

A black and white video was frozen on the monitor. The view was from across the street from the El Camino. Collins was shown halfway out of her car.

"A number of houses on that cul-de-sac had security systems that included video. It's a nice neighbourhood. I guess they wanted to keep it that way. I grabbed as much video as I could. Came in early this morning to look at them and found this."

"Oh, for Christ's sake, Hastings. What are we

looking at?"

"Relax, Cap." Hastings hit the space bar and started the video.

Collins walks around the back of the El Camino and squares off with the mystery woman. Collins raises her gun and as she pulls the trigger she's hit with the Taser. Her arm jerks and -

Hastings tapped the space bar and paused the video. "That tree? Techs pulled the slug out of it that matched ballistics for those cases on the board."

Hastings paused and wiped his mouth. "I can't explain it. And I really don't believe it, but," he pointed at the monitor, "Collins' gun was used in all of these killings." He held up his hands. "Hang on, that's not accurate. The ballistics don't match her service revolver. But they do match the weapon used in these killings."

Chapter 37

Barnes covered his mouth. "Jesus Christ."

Hastings popped the space bar. "That's not all of it."

Collins writhes on the road. The El Camino jumps the curb and speeds out of frame. Collins crawls to her car.

Hastings froze the video again. He zoomed to the weapon in her hand. "That, gentlemen, is not her service revolver. That is the murder weapon. In Collins' hand." He restarted the video.

Collins stretches into her car and deposits the Beretta and suppressor in her glove box, then collapses on the road beside her car.

Hastings stopped the video. "I can't believe it, but this doesn't lie. And it hasn't been doctored. Raw footage from the home-owners sent directly to me.”

Collins sat in her car in the parking lot, waiting for the engine to warm up. Frost coated the outside of the windshield. She opened the glove box and rummaged through the mess, pushing the Beretta to one side and extracted an ice scraper. She looked at it, then at the frost slowly melting in ever-increasing semi-circles and tossed the scraper back in the glove box.

She ducked down, looking through the cleared gap on the windshield, trying to determine if it was cleared enough to drive yet, when her phone rang. She looked at the display. “Damn.” She poked the green button. “How's it going, Cap? I've left the station. You don't have to worry about me.”

“I'm looking at a picture here, Collins, and it doesn't look good.”

“Ah, shit. You caught me stealing sugar packets from the lunchroom. I thought I got away with it.” She folded an arm across her chest. “Or is it something else?"

"You shot the tree. You shot the tree with the same gun that shot Wheeler. You need to get back in here and provide me with a compelling explanation or I'm going to have to arrest you. I don't want to arrest you, Collins."

Collins looked at the open glove box, and the butt of the Beretta, and closed her eyes.

"Maybe ballistics fucked up, Captain. It's happened before."

"I've got video. Get in here. Don't make me wait. I'd hate to have to go get you."

Collins looked at her phone, shook her head and hung up. "Shit."

Hastings sat at his desk, looking at a screen grab of Collins shoving the Beretta into her glove box. "What in the hell, Collins? What in the everlasting, mother-fucking hell?" He looked through the glass walls of the War Room at Barnes and Wilson in animated discussion. Barnes shook his head and pushed past Wilson. He targeted Hastings' desk.

Wilson was close on his heels. "Captain Barnes, we need to bring her in."

Barnes ignored him and slammed the same grainy photo Hastings was looking at on Hastings' desk. "Have you talked to her yet? She hung up on me. She needs to get her ass in here NOW and explain this."

Wilson shoved his head in. "She's our-"

"Shut the fuck up, Wilson, and get back in your fucking room."

Wilson took a half step back, his hands on his hips. "But-"

"Hastings, get her on the fucking phone and get her in here now."

"Ah, shit." Hastings' watched Barnes storm back up to his office.

Wilson hovered by Hastings' desk. "Put her on speaker."

"She's not the serial killer, you idiot. I'm sure there's

a very good explanation for what we saw. Let me talk to her. She probably doesn't trust you and your team."

"You're on the team."

"Not by choice." Hastings sighed and poked the speaker button on his desk phone. "Dial it down a bit, Wilson. She's been a cop longer than you've worn long pants." He dialed her number and sat back in his chair as it rang.

Collins parked and was walking up the front steps to her apartment when her phone rang. She stopped on the steps and answered. "What now, Hastings?"

"Got you on speaker. Wilson's with me."

"Lucky me." Collins looked at her apartment, then back at her car. She retraced her steps and got back in and started it.

"Where are you now?"

"I've got some leave built up, Hastings. I'm going to take it. Those Taser barbs took more out of me than I thought they did." She jammed the phone between her jaw and shoulder as she pulled from the curb. "So if you don't mind, I haven't been to Florida in years. Too hot in summer. I think I'll head there today."

"Listen, Detective, I need you to come in and -"

"Wilson, I don't work for you. Go fu-find someone else to bother."

"I don't appreciate the tone, Detective," said Wilson. "You're a suspect now."

Collins laughed. "You have video of me shooting anyone other than the fucking tree?" She chewed her lip. "I got that gun off the killer behind the pool hall. Stupid that I didn't report it, but I make no apologies."

"That's horseshit, Collins. I've worked beside you for almost a decade and you're not *that* stupid. You think you can do a better job than the FBI, well, so do I. But there are procedures we have to follow and you know it."

Collins smiled and parked about a block from the El Camino house and got out of her car. "Love you too, Hastings. Give me a bit of space, okay? I've got some things to do. Then we'll talk."

Wilson's voice came over the line. "That's not how it works, Detective. You're a real suspect in this. You don't come in, I'm going to have to send someone to get you. And you won't like that."

"Tough guy. I told you, give me a couple of hours." Collins hung up, went to throw her phone as far as she could, then stopped, looked at it, and slipped it in her pocket. She took the Beretta and silencer from the glove box and locked the doors and threw the keys into the long grass on the side of the road.

Hastings looked at the phone and ran his fingers through his hair. "Jesus."

"You going to launch the hounds, or will I?" Wilson leaned forward and got in Hastings' face. "Push back on this and I'll charge you as a co-conspirator."

Chapter 38

Collins looked back at her car, then turned her back on it. She shoved her hands in her pockets and walked the block to the house.

She locked the door behind her and entered the garage, bumped the shelf and rode down to the lower level.

She ran her hand along the side of the car. "Sweet, sweet ride. Shame to get rid of you." She got in, rolled down the window and backed onto the lowered floor. She reached out the window and poked the button that raised her into the garage.

She lowered the visor and found the garage door opener. "Gonna keep you." She pushed the button and watched in the side mirror as the door rose. When it was up far enough to get the car out she reversed into the driveway and pushed the button again, then dropped the opener in her pocket.

"Okay. Where do I stash you?"

Barnes stood at the front of the War Room. "Full court press, people. Her apartment, and coffee shops or bars she's known to frequent. Hastings, you get the tech working on finding her phone.

"There's a BOLO out for her and her car. Be gentle with her. She's been on the force almost thirty years."

Wilson bristled. "Captain Barnes, she doesn't get special-"

"Shut up Wilson, or go home." Barnes addressed the remainder of the room. "No rough stuff. She's at the end of her career and probably feels like she's being carted off to pasture against her will. You find her, call me and see if you can sit down and have a chat with her. If she takes off, keep a loose tail."

Wilson glared at Barnes and walked to the back of

the room, his mobile stuck to the side of his head.

Collins drove through a neighborhood that had suffered the worst of the economic recession. More than half of the houses were abandoned and wrecked beyond rehabilitation. Many of those occupied were not occupied by their rightful owners, which at this point would have been a bank or other financial institution.

She drove to the middle of the block and pulled to the curb. A couple of young urban entrepreneurs sat on the front steps of one of the houses. She looked in her rearview mirror and saw someone who was probably one of their colleagues about three houses down, sitting on the front step and keeping lookout.

One of the guys walked over to the car and leaned in the passenger's side window. "You a cop?"

"Why would you think I was a cop?"

"Nice white lady in a neighborhood like this, in a car like that, you're sure as hell not a customer."

"That's pretty racist. For a white guy."

The guy looked to his left and nodded. Collins looked in the rearview mirror and saw the lookout slide something in the back of his baggy pants and sit back on the steps.

"So what you looking for, pretty lady? Some weed? You look like you're old enough to have enjoyed the hippy life. Plenty nicer places to get weed, though. Not safe around here."

"Not looking for weed. Or ice or crank or horse or blow or whatever else is on your menu." She smiled at the guy and popped open her glove box. "Not looking for you either, so relax." She pulled the Beretta out of the glove box and held it with her index finger through the trigger guard.

She eased out of the driver's side of the car and looked over the hood at the young man's gun barrel. "I said relax, right? I'm not after you. And I don't care about your drugs. You'll wipe yourself out in a couple of years, anyway." She removed the silencer and dropped it her jacket pocket. She holstered the Beretta on her ankle and stood.

She took out her phone. "Give me a minute. I've got to make a call."

The drug dealer held his gun beside his leg and watched as Collins dialed.

"That you, Collins?"

"It is, Geez. What you up to?"

"Tryna sleep. What time is it?"

Collins scratched her chin. "I'm looking for that El Camino again. Put the word out. If one of your guys finds it, call Hastings, okay? I'm going off the grid for a little while."

"Who's Hastings?"

"One of the -" she looked at the drug dealer, "-guys I work with."

"Yeah, I don't got his number."

"I'll send it to you. Hundred bucks in it for you." She hung up and sent a text to Geezer. She looked at her phone and tossed it in through the car window.

"You don't want that?"

"No, and you don't either." She took out the Beretta. "Relax." She opened the door and stuffed it under the driver's seat. "This car is going to be really hot in a few hours. If you're going to take it, make sure you get it off the street before the cops find it. And they'll be looking for it." She tossed him the keys. "Don't say I didn't warn you."

"What the hell?"

Collins winked at him. "I'll see you around, no doubt."

She slid her hands in her pockets and started walking.

Hastings hung up his phone. "I just got a call from one of Collins' confidential informants. He told me that she wanted him to call me if he tracked down the El Camino. She's still tracking that woman."

Wilson dropped a file folder on his desk. "So why'd she want him to call you?"

Hastings shrugged. "She's still on this vendetta thing, but wants us to back her up." He pointed at Wilson. "How long have you been looking for this car, and one of her CI's found it in an hour. Maybe we wouldn't be having this problem if she was on this task force from the very beginning." Hastings grabbed his jacket. "Let's go."

Collins walked with a steady pace. It felt good. Almost an hour of steady walking and relatively fresh air and she hadn't felt this invigorated in years. She estimated that she had walked almost six miles. Her cheeks were stiff from the cold, but she didn't feel it. "The old girl was right. I need to hit the gym. It's been too long."

She walked around the corner to the street she lived on, about two blocks from her apartment building, and spotted a parked car idling a block from her home. She slowed and leaned against a tree.

She flipped her jacket hood up and looked around.

On the other side of the street, a little closer to the apartment building, a black and white was pulled up in a driveway. "Ain't no such thing as coincidences."

She hunched her shoulders into her jacket and turned on her heels. "A little bit more exercise never hurt anybody."

Hastings looked at the two guys sitting on the front step, who in turn were watching him. He got out of the car and walked over to them. "Beautiful day, boys. You been sitting here long?"

"What's it to you?"

"I'm homicide, not vice. Your drugs are somebody else's problem, not mine. I'm looking for a black El Camino. I was told it was left here."

The guy shrugged. "Don't see one around here. Do you?"

Hastings held out his phone with Collins' ID photo on the screen. "You seen this woman around?"

The dealer looked at the picture, then smiled at

Hastings. "Little old lady evading justice? What'd she do?"

"She's a detective. Homicide. I think she may be in trouble."

The dealer looked up the street in the direction Collins had walked, then back at Hastings. "Never saw the lady." The dealer looked around. "Now if you could fuck off, you're hurting business."

Hastings chuckled. "My friend, someone will be by later. You might want to close up shop and get the hell out of here."

The dealer looked around. "You think the neighbors mind?" He shuffled back to the front step and sat. "The lady was tough. Be careful."

Chapter 39

Hastings got back in his car. He looked over at Wilson. "What?"

"Lost her again? She's making you look like a fool."

"And how's the task force doing? I get why she doesn't like you guys now." He opened his phone and called the station. "Detective Hastings for the tech guys."

He looked at Wilson while he waited and shook his head. "She found the car in an hour." He returned to the phone "Hey, techs. Have you tracked Collins' phone yet?"

"This is Detective Hastings?"

"Yeah. We're on a time limit here, guys. Where's the phone?"

"It was turned off about an hour ago."

"Send me its last location." Hastings hung up and waited for the message. The address linked to the map app on his phone and resolved to a spot about fifteen feet behind him. "Shit."

"What?"

Hastings handed his phone to Wilson. "She must have dumped the phone with the car."

Wilson pointed out the window. "Those guys weren't helpful?"

Hastings looked at the two on the front step. "Nope." He picked the mic off the dash. "Detective Hastings for the uniforms in front of Collins' apartment building. Has there been any sign of her?"

"Dead as a doornail here, Detective."

"Thanks." Hastings reattached the mic to the dash. He looked at Wilson. "Any ideas?"

"Get the last twenty-four hours of phone locations. There'll be a pattern."

Collins sprinted around the corner and took a bead on the house. She heard sirens behind her, and coincidence was definitely not a thing. She grabbed the garage remote from her pocket and pressed the button repeatedly. "Shit. Open, open, open."

She got close enough to be in range and the door started rising, then stopped and lowered as she continued to mash the button. "Shit."

She pressed it again as she ran up the driveway, hit the ground and rolled under the rising door. She hit the button again, closing it.

A black and white, with lights on and sirens loud, screeched to a stop at the bottom of the driveway.

Collins hit the shelf on the wall and rode the floor down. "Faster. Must go faster." She looked up into the garage, listening to the cars accumulating outside.

When it was halfway down, she jumped off into the cavern below. She smashed the button on the wall and watched the floor rise back into place.

When it stopped at the top, she looked at her watch,

grabbed a juice pack and a newspaper. All the news fit to print for July 9th, 1997.

Hastings and Wilson stopped beside one of the black and whites. "This is one of the locations she's been at the last couple of days." He jumped out of his car and corralled a uniformed officer. "Where are we at with this?"

"First at the scene saw her roll into the garage. We're about to go in."

Hastings walked up the front steps. "Have you knocked?" He rapped on the door. "Who owns this place?"

"We're still trying to find that out, detective."

Hastings knocked on the door again. "Police. We've got a few questions, Collins. Open, or we knock the door down."

Collins heard the door smash open and feet trundle across the floor above her head. She tapped the spacebar on the keyboard and brought the monitors to life. She crumpled the juice box and threw it in the trash and started exploring the area.

It was clearly a temporary accommodation. A wardrobe stood in the corner, beside the cot. She opened the door and pulled out a pair of dark track pants and a black hoodie.

"Deja vu. Damn."

She pulled on the track pants and hoodie and looked down at herself. "Well, I'll be damned."

Footsteps moved into the garage area. She froze and looked up, then sat in front of the monitors. Voices carried from the space above her. She watched the flashlight beams crisscross the garage on the monitor.

"So tell me where in the hell she went," said Hastings.

"We're still looking, Detective."

"It's not a very big house, Constable. Take it apart."

Wilson grumbled something Collins couldn't hear, then said, "So who in the - who owns this place?"

"We're working on it, dammit," said Hastings. "But I don't give a fuck who owns it. Where is she?"

Collins smiled and leaned back in the chair. Her chair. She grabbed another juice pack. It'd be a couple more hours. She picked through a stack of books on the table and pulled one out that promised adventures with aliens and wormholes in Australia.

Chapter 40

Collins stood and rolled the kinks out of her neck. She looked at her watch and swore. "Three hours? Jesus." She cocked an ear and listened. The house was dead quiet.

She checked the monitors. All clear. She held her hand in front of the big red button for a second, then took a deep breath and pressed it.

The floor slowly lowered with a deep rumble. She stepped to one side and held her hand near the button.

The floor reached the bottom, and silence returned. She waited for a second then stepped on to the floor and popped the button again. She rose with it into the garage.

She walked into the house, a little more casual. A

quick check of the rooms confirmed that the house was empty. She walked to the front window and peered through the venetian blinds. A black and white car idled at the curb. She stepped back and took a deep breath.

"Now's as good a time as any."

She pulled the piece of notepaper out of her pocket and walked to the larger bedroom. She tipped up the hanger and pulled on the closet rod. The back wall slowly dropped, exposing the glass-domed chair. She pressed her hand on the panel and a low humming accompanied the rising of the dome.

She sat in the chair and looked at the list. "Will Davidson. Kiddie-porn production. May 12, 1992." Her fingers hovered over the keypad. "I'm going to need a couple of days to get a car and gun."

She entered 1992-05-10 05:00 and pressed "enter". The dome lowered.

She disappeared among the electrical arcs.

About the Author

Tony McFadden is a displaced Canadian now calling Australia home. He and his wife and two children live near the beaches where he spends as much time as possible writing.

More about Tony and his writing can be found at TonyMcFadden.net/mybooks, Facebook and Twitter (Yes. I still call it Twitter)

Also by Tony McFadden

Hollyweird	⇒	G'Day LA
	⇒	G'Day USA
Matt Daly's Adventures	⇒	Matt's War
	⇒	Daly Battles: The Fall of Pyongyang
	⇒	Target: Australia
The Miami Mob	⇒	Book 'Em – An Eamonn Shute Mystery
	⇒	Unprotected Sax
	⇒	Family Matters
The Sci-Fi	⇒	Have Wormhole, Will Travel
	⇒	Killing Time
Mac D Cases	⇒	Mac D: Private Investigator
	⇒	A Step Too Far
	⇒	Hunter / Prey
McGinnis Investigations	⇒	The Murder of Jeremy Brookes
	⇒	Number Fifteen
Nick Harding Cases	⇒	Batteries Not Included
	⇒	Broken
	⇒	Dead Tomorrow
	⇒	Under the Shadows